BOOKS BY KRISTIE COOK

SOUL SAVERS

Recommended Reading Order:

A Demon's Promise

An Angel's Purpose

Genesis: A Soul Savers Novella

Dangerous Devotion

Dark Power

Sacred Wrath

Unholy Torment

Fractured Faith

Age of Angels Part I: Awakened

Age of Angels Part II: Lost

Age of Angels Part III: Marked

Prophecy of the Wolves: (A Soul Savers Tie-In Novella)

Wonder: A Soul Savers Collection of Holiday Short Stories & Recipes

HAVENWOOD FALLS

Recommended Reading Order:

Forget You Not

Lose You Not

Break Me Not

The Collector: Awakening

Savage Salvation (Sin & Silk)

Sun & Moon Academy Book One: Fall Semester

Sun & Moon Academy Book Two: Fall Semester

SOUL SAVERS BOOK 8

AGE OF ANGELS

PART 1: AWAKENED

KRISTIE COOK

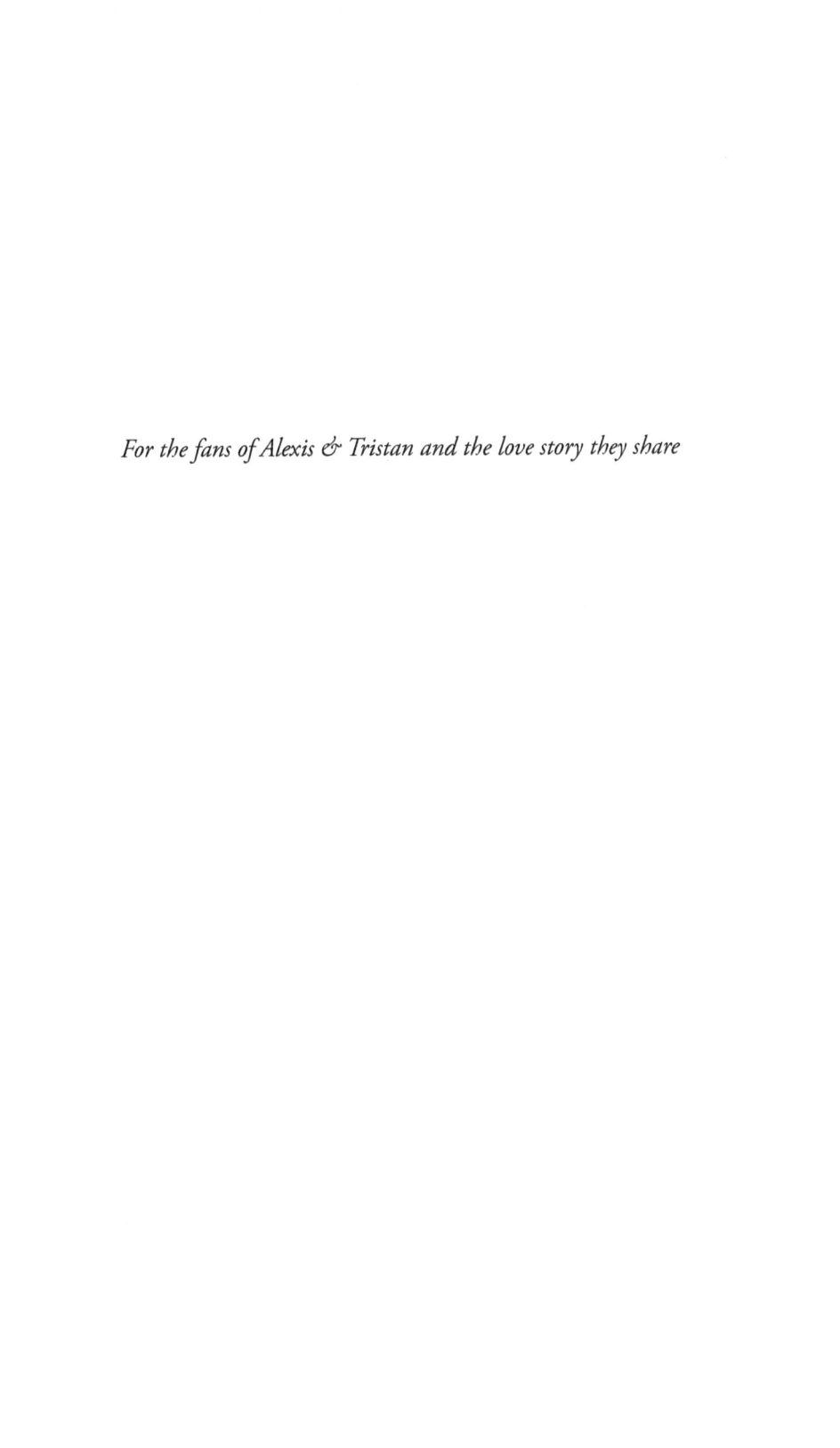

For the fans of Alexis & Tristan and the love story they share

CHAPTER 1

*W*hispered voices filter through the watery realm of semiconsciousness and grow louder the closer I rise to the surface. Anxiety fills their muffled tones, both male and female. My body shakes, and sharp points dig into my back. The side of my face suddenly lights up with a sting.

"Tell me you did not just slap her," a male voice accuses.

"She needs to wake the hell up." The female reply sounds like music, even in its harshness.

"Vanessa, you can't go around slapping our matriarch," another woman's voice reprimands.

The first one huffs. "She'll get over it and then probably slap me back."

As my fingers brush over my cheek, I try to open my eyes. My lids feel heavy and scratchy, but I manage a slit. Sunlight glares, and they shut again on their own. With a few flutters against the light, I finally focus on the scene before me. Or rather, above me. I'm lying on the ground with three faces hovering over me—two females and a male—and behind them gleams the sun through an entanglement of bare tree branches.

Where am I? What happened?

"See? It worked," says the musical voice. My gaze finds her stunning face with skin nearly as white as her hair that's pulled back into a tight ponytail. Her light blue eyes, however, are like ice daggers as they glower at me. But they fail to pierce through the fog in my mind. "Come on, your highness. Enough of the dramatics. Get up. We need to get out of here."

A pale hand wraps around my upper arm before I can move, and I flinch.

"Vanessa," the other female admonishes again, her brown hair hanging around her face as she looks down at me. Her breath plumes in a thin fog as she speaks. She places a long, thin hand over the first and pulls it away. "Give her a minute. She passed out."

"We don't have a minute," Vanessa growls. "And she's fine now."

"Sheree's right," the guy says. Worry etches three lines between his sapphire eyes as he studies me. He rubs his chin covered with thick scruff, which is a slightly darker hue than the straw-colored hair sticking out from under his knit cap. "She looks out of it. Alexis, are you okay? It's me, Owen. Can you see me?"

I blink, frown, and try to sit up. My vision wavers, and I close my eyes for a moment, pressing my fingers to my lids. *What the hell has happened to me?* I slowly open them again. Everyone's stepped back to give me space, but their gazes remain heavily on me. I swallow, or try to. My throat feels like sandpaper. I lick my lips, tasting the slightly bitter odor hanging in the air, but the effort is pointless, my tongue as dry as my throat.

"Thirsty," I manage to croak out.

"Aren't we all," someone else mutters.

My perspective shifts outward to find two other men beyond the circle around me, both dressed in thick parkas, knit hats, and gloves. They're armed with a crossbow and a gun that they keep in ready position as they each make a slow circle, watching the woods surrounding the clearing where we're gathered. The trees are half brown and half gray, with a few withered leaves fluttering from some of the branches as though hanging on even in death. Most branches, however, are bare. Something about them seems odd, as though the limbs aren't naked only because of the time of year, but for another reason. I can't pinpoint what I feel like I should know through my hazy mind. Off to my left, the surface of a large lake glitters in the sun, the far shore barely visible in the distance. I gnaw on my lip. I have no idea where I am.

"What happened?" I ask as I rise to my feet.

Vanessa's hand darts out to help me, her touch cold as ice. I withdraw my arm from her hold as soon as I'm standing and take a step back. Her eyes narrow as they visually assess my condition, the look in them causing a shiver down my spine.

"Are you sure you're okay?" Sheree's upper body leans toward me, and her head tilts. Her brown-eyed gaze never leaves my face, looking down at me from her much taller height. She has to be nearly six feet tall, her body rail thin and all legs in her cutoff denim shorts. A thick belt cinches the waist, a long knife hanging from it. She probably has another in one of her combat boots. Weapons hang from all kinds of places on everyone in the group, including me.

I press my fingers to my aching temples and rub circles into them. "No, not really."

"Awesome," Owen mutters as his long leg kicks a small rock across the clearing. "It's gotta be dark magic messing with your head, too deep for me to reach."

"This is your fault," Vanessa snaps at him. "I can't believe you let her drink the water."

He rolls his eyes as his hands drop to his hips. "It's not like I didn't try to stop her. Besides, you know how she is. She does what she wants. If she wants to test the water herself before anyone else does, she's gonna do it."

"God forbid anyone else take a risk." Vanessa's voice changes to a higher pitch, mocking. "They might die, so I better do it instead."

Owen snorts, and the other guys in the group chuckle.

Sheree frowns. "Hey, be nice. That's who she is. She wouldn't ask anyone to do what she won't do herself. That's why she's here. Right, Alexis?"

My brow furrows as they all stare at me again, and I rub the back of my neck. "I have no idea what you're talking about."

"Of course you don't," Vanessa quips. "Come on. Let's get the hell out of here before more of those little needle things start flying again. Whatever the hell they are."

"We need to get these water samples back ASAP," Owen agrees.

Sheree glances at me sideways. "Looking at Alexis, I'm not so sure about that water."

Owen lifts a brow and holds his hands up, wiggling his fingers. "Do you doubt my magical abilities, woman? It'll be as pristine as newly fallen snow by the time I'm done with it."

The guy with the crossbow chuffs. "I don't think newly fallen snow is so clean anymore. It was blue last time."

"And purple the time before that," the other guy adds.

3

Vanessa gives an impatient flick of her hand as she settles her gaze on Owen. "Are you going to make a portal or what?"

"What about our search for the others?" Sheree asks. "Are we giving up on them?"

Everyone turns and looks at me expectantly. I stare back at them, not understanding what they want. My thoughts bounce all over the place from trying to follow their conversation.

Vanessa sighs and shakes her head. "Let's get the hell going."

She strides out of the clearing and into the woods as though everyone would automatically follow, and pretty much everyone does. All but Owen and me. Sheree looks over her shoulder at me and stops.

"Aren't you coming?"

I shake my head. Is she crazy?

"Do you want to portal back then?" she asks.

When I don't answer, Sheree and Owen exchange a look. The others stop their movement into the woods.

"Damn water." Owen gestures toward the lake. "What the heck did it do to you?"

"What do you mean?" I ask.

"I thought I hit the bottle out of your hand, but you dropped to the ground like a stone, lights out for a good two minutes. And now look at you. You're all whacked out."

"Whacked out?" I echo.

"Disoriented." Sheree joins us back in the clearing. "Right? That's how you feel?"

I squeeze the back of my neck again as I glance around. "That's one word for it."

"Hopefully, that's all it's done to you, and there's no other damage," Sheree says. "Does everything else feel okay?"

I look down at my black boots, leather-clad legs, and torso barely covered in a tight-fitting tank top. A dagger hangs from a belt on my right hip, and a knife is strapped to my left leg. Everything seems to be in order. No pains or aches anywhere but in my brain. "Yeah, I think so. It's just my head."

Owen shifts his weight. "I tried to pull the black magic out of you when you went down, but there's apparently something I can't reach alone. Let's get you home, and Blossom can help figure this out."

"Home . . ." I can't picture home. My mind comes up completely blank.

"You know, The Loft?" Sheree says. "Where Tristan and the babies are, and the rest of our people?"

"The place we've called home for over a year now." Vanessa returns to the clearing, too. Annoyance crosses her face when I show no recognition. "You know, since that day Lucas and the Demons pretty much destroyed the world with their nuclear and magic bombs?"

My gaze swings to the trees. That's what I'd noticed to be wrong with them—many of them lack any color at all, even what remains of the leaves. Barely a trace of orange or even brown. I squint my eyes as I look out at the lake and the surrounding land. Lots of gray out there, too. Not all of it, however, as though color has slowly seeped into the landscape. Winter colors, though, except for some scattered specks of pink and yellow on the ground and tree trunks. Is that some kind of pollen? In the middle of winter?

Owen moves his hand closer to my back, a familiar yet hands-off gesture to move along. "Come on. We'll get you all fixed up, and the whole hellish story will come back to you."

My muscles stiffen, though, as a small stick, like a miniature arrow or a long needle, whizzes by my nose. A poof of colored dust trails behind it, although none of it lands on us, as if we're each encased in an invisible bubble. Several more needles sail through the air around us.

"There they are again! What the fuck *are* they?" Vanessa takes off, running in the direction the sticks had come from.

Owen, however, somehow swoops me into his thickly muscled arms before I know what's happening and sprints the opposite way.

"What the hell are you doing?" I yell and kick and squirm, the rough wool of his sweater scraping against my bare skin.

"I need to get you home."

"The hell you are. Put me down!"

"I'm not fighting you on this. Tristan will—"

"I said to put me down!" With a burst of energy, I spring free from his arms.

At the same time, a ripping sound comes from behind me, large, dark shapes explode from my back, and I sail into the air, high out of Owen's reach. I look over my shoulder and gasp. Purple and black wings spread out to span nearly five feet from each side of me. Although somewhere in the back of my mind I must have known they were there—that they're a part of me—their unexpected appearance takes me by surprise.

"Come on, Alexis," Owen growls as I hang in the air above him. "That's not fair."

He lifts his palm up toward me as though it's some kind of threat. With a mere thought, the wings bat against the air, and I rise higher until I hit the tree branches and careen back to the ground. I barely adjust my legs in time to land in a crouch.

Owen steps toward me.

"Stay back," I warn.

"Then pull yourself together and let's go," he counters.

"I'm not going anywhere with you!"

Owen takes another step closer. I draw the dagger from the sheath on my hip. I bend my knees, coiling my muscles, and hold the blade between us.

"Leave me alone!"

He moves to take another step, and I twitch the blade. His deep-blue eyes narrow.

"Alexis . . ."

I rock forward on the balls of my feet.

"Seriously?" He lifts a blond brow. "I'm not going to fight you."

I glare at him, dagger still out, and then my gaze bounces to the others who've come up behind him. They all look at me like I've lost my mind. Maybe I have. But they also carefully watch me as though I'm a wild animal. And that's okay. If I scare them enough, they'll leave me alone and go back to their so-called home. As if anyone has a home anymore.

"I lost them, whatever they are." Vanessa runs back over, so fast her body's nearly a blur. "They must have flashed because they disappeared. Come on. Let's get the hell out of here."

When she stops, she glances at everyone, her eyes landing on me while I brandish a weapon at her companions. She blows out an annoyed huff.

"Enough of this. We're taking you home."

I don't see her move, but she instantly has an arm braced around me like a steel bar locking me against her body. She carries me through the woods at an unnatural speed, the trees blurring by us. I thrash against her and dig the tip of the dagger across her forearm. She doesn't even flinch, and the wound closes up right away. I kick her shins and throw an elbow into her ribs. Her hold loosens. I seize the opportunity and twist free, landing on my feet, dagger pointed at her. She stops in her tracks, and everyone else does, too, as they approach from behind her.

"I'm not going anywhere with you," I snarl once again. "Who the hell do you think you are to expect me to? I don't know where I am or who I am, and I certainly don't know any of you!"

CHAPTER 2

*T*he admission flies out of my mouth before I can stop it. I've been trying to hide my loss of memory from them, not wanting to show these people any vulnerability. But I'll be damned if I go anywhere with them! Not by choice nor by force.

No, I need time. Time to figure out who I am, where I am, and where I'm supposed to be. Time to remember . . .

I haven't forgotten everything, of course. Bits and pieces of knowledge and information remain. I mean, I obviously know how to walk, how to talk, and how to defend myself. At least, by instinct, if not by training. I have wings, but I don't remember how to use them, which is baffling since I use my legs and arms fine. I apparently know my words and have no issues with communication. My brain functions on some level much higher than an infant's. That's the good news.

I can't grasp a single memory from my past, though. No history, as though my life began when I woke up ten minutes ago. Except . . . I somehow know the world has changed, that it had been different than it is now, but I have no idea how or why. I know being on the Earth's surface is dangerous, that anything could kill you, including the monsters—both Earthly and Otherworldly—roaming the land. I know this is a post-apocalyptic life of survival.

But I don't know my own name, who I am, if I'm supposed to be alone or if other people are searching for me. I definitely don't know this group who found me, who act like they know me, even gave me the name Alexis.

But for all I know, they're simply trying to con me. You can't trust anyone anymore. Maybe you never could.

The strangers stare at me as I hold my dagger out, some with disbelief written on their faces, others with suspicion in their eyes. I wish they'd move on and leave me alone, but they're determined to take me with them.

"What the fuck do you mean, you don't know us?" Vanessa demands. *Vampire.* The word pops into my head out of nowhere as I glare at her, and right after it, the realization that she is one. Vampires are one of the creatures that ended the world. I don't know how I know any of this, but I do, in my gut. "We're all practically family!"

I shake my head, not believing her lies.

"Oh, this is lovely." She stomps her heel into the ground and throws her hands in the air. They land back on her hips.

"Tristan's so going to kill us," mutters one of the guys who isn't Owen.

"No shit. I don't want to be around when he finds out," says the other one.

"We just need to get her home safe, and we'll figure it out," Sheree says. She's supernatural, I decide, based on her unseasonal clothing and the vibe I get from her, although she doesn't feel like a vampire. *What is she?*

The first guy, probably a normal human since he's dressed appropriately for the weather, snorts. "I still don't want to be there. That dude is scary as shit when he wants to be."

Vanessa turns to Owen. "He's going to be so pissed at you. We could bail, you know. Make a portal and be halfway around the world."

I can tell by the look she gives him that there's something going on between them. Something about that seems weird to me. He's tall, nicely built, and not bad looking at all, although he does nothing for me. She's gorgeous with curves in all the right places and could have been a model in a past life. But it's more than their appearances that doesn't seem to quite match. Something about them . . .

"Moose doesn't scare me." Owen takes several steps toward me, his hand reaching out for my arm, and I snap back to attention. "Let's get you home."

I flick my wrist, waving the knife toward him. "Nuh-uh. Stay back. I told you. I'm not going anywhere with you."

"Uh, yeah. You are." Vanessa also moves for me.

Are they seriously going to abduct me? Well, of course they are. Owen has already tried. They're going to take me away from wherever I'm *supposed* to be. Which is . . . I have no idea. But surely I'm supposed to be somewhere. Surely someone's looking for me. Right? Or am I left alone in this world? Ugh! Why the hell can't I remember? And what could they possibly want with me? What value do I hold to them?

"You're our leader. Our matriarch. You *have* to go with us," Sheree says.

I barely suppress a laugh. That's a little over the top. No, *way* over the top. Who do they think they're kidding? I may have lost my memories, but I'm not stupid. Their leader? Ha! But they'd probably tell me anything to convince me to go with them without a fight. But a fight is what they're going to get if they don't leave me the hell alone.

Before anyone can make another move, a huge, dark shadow passes over us and a horrible screeching fills my head. Everyone looks up, and after taking a quick glance of my own, I run. I don't know what that thing is, but I'm pretty sure I don't want to. I race through the woods, hurdling underbrush and fallen trees and ducking under low limbs, running away from the strangers as much as from the beast in the sky. The wings do me absolutely no good, hindering my escape as stray branches catch on them. I wish they'd go away, and they do. I still feel their presence, but they're no longer visible and no longer in the way. I run faster.

A stream of fire shoots down from above, lighting up a dead tree a few yards ahead of me. I pivot to my left, away from the lake, and continue storming my way through the forest. More little needle-things zoom by my head, leaving a trail of pink and yellow dust on the ground. Shouts come from behind me as well as what sounds like crashing trees, but I don't hear anyone directly on my heels.

Yet, suddenly I'm thrown forward into a tree trunk.

"You are *not* pulling this shit on my watch," Vanessa snarls as I spin around.

She comes at me again, and with the dagger still in my hand, I jump up and lunge at her. We tumble to the ground together and roll around as she tries to pin me down and I fight her off. Knowing she's a vampire, I expect her to easily take me down, but I'm able to hold my own. So what does that make me? I can't worry about that now. I find an opportunity and manage to shove my boots into her pelvis and throw her off of me. I spring to my feet. We glare at each other for about a second. If my blade had connected at all, there are no signs of damage to her perfect porcelain skin. She must have already healed. Definitely a vampire. After that one second pause, we both spring into the air and lunge at each other.

But this time, we freeze in mid-motion.

I try with all my might and determination to move, but I have no control over any part of my body. I'm completely paralyzed, can't even set my foot on the ground for balance. How do I not topple over? Vanessa blows out a sharp breath, and her eyes roll upward.

"Shit," she mutters under her breath. "You should've just come with me."

Okay, so we're not completely paralyzed. We can move our mouths and eyes. I look up to follow her gaze. A large figure descends on us.

A man, powerfully built, with wings like mine, but black and silver rather than black and purple. And he obviously knows how to use them, unlike me. He's not the same beast I'd seen in the sky moments ago. That hadn't been a man at all, and its wings had been shaped differently. This guy, or whatever he is, lands in front of us, and the sight of him takes my breath.

Partly because of the power he exudes that leaves me feeling more vulnerable than ever. And partly because of how his tall, muscular frame strains against the black, sleeveless T-shirt and how he perfectly fills out the black leather pants. Then there's his face, framed by shoulder-length, sandy brown hair. His features are inhumanly beautiful with a chiseled jaw and full lips, neither of which could be hidden under a few days' worth of stubble. He has a face like you'd expect of an angel. But more than any of that, what really traps the air in my lungs, are his eyes as they lock on mine. Emerald green with brown and gold around the pupils and framed with long, dark lashes. They capture me . . . enrapture me. Even as they slowly travel down my body and back up again, sending tingles throughout every nerve of my body.

The feeling of helplessness escalates to a frightening level. I swear he knows everything about me with that slow inspection—that my heart hammers painfully against my ribs, that my insides flutter and flare with heat at the same time, that my nipples have grown hard against my top. Well, he could probably see that perfectly fine through the thin fabric of the tank I wear. And I can't move my arms to hide them.

His eyes narrow as they return to my face and then move to Vanessa.

"Care to tell me what the hell's going on here?" he demands, his voice low and hard, making me quiver with both fear and intrigue.

I try to move again, but I'm still paralyzed. His large hand, which he'd been holding up in the air, drifts to his side. At the same time, I lose my balance and fall to the ground. Vanessa drops to her feet, landing with the grace of an elite dancer.

"Hold on to her," she warns, but she's too late.

I spring up and sprint away, but I don't go very far. I'm paralyzed again, caught in mid-step. I roar a string of profanities as the feeling of vulnerability enrages me. How is this happening? It can't be the same magic that took my memory, because Vanessa had been stuck, too. She's not now, though . . .

"What happened?" the winged man asks again as he and Vanessa appear in front of me. Hard eyes glare at me, a fierce stare that elicits a chill up my spine. "I felt your mind close off from mine, our connection cut. You never opened it back up."

"She doesn't remember us," Vanessa answers although I think he'd been talking to me.

Not that I can answer. I don't understand what he means, but even if I did, I don't think my mouth would work. My brain's barely functioning in his presence.

"She doesn't seem to remember anything," Vanessa continues, "including that she can fly or flash, thank the Angels."

The beautiful man cocks his head as a small smile turns up one side of his mouth. "Surely, you remember me."

Or maybe it's an arrogant smirk.

I try to shake my head in response, but can't. My throat and jaw work to answer, and my voice comes out small under his piercing stare. "No."

The smirk disappears as his brows draw together, and he steps closer to me. His hand lifts toward my face, and my body trembles against whatever has me paralyzed. Then I realize *he* has me paralyzed, a special power he must possess. Is he really some kind of Angel? I sort of remember . . . something about Angels. Something that dangles on the very far outreaches of my memory, but not within grasp.

When his fingertips touch my cheek, electricity shoots through my entire body, and I yelp. Some kind of feeling of familiarity briefly tugs at my mind but disappears faster than it came. The man frowns, and the pain that shines in his eyes sends a crack into my heart. Although I haven't done anything to cause the look, not that I know of, I so badly want to fix it for him.

"Where's Owen?" he asks, his voice a low growl.

"Right here." Owen appears next to the Angel dude, seeming

somewhat smaller now in comparison. "I tried to knock the water out of her hands, dude, I swear, but I think some might have got on her anyway. In her."

The Angel guy growls again, but it's loud and frightening, more like a feral roar. Out of my peripheral vision, I watch both Vanessa and Owen exchange a glance as they slink several steps backward. I can almost hear Vanessa telling Owen, "I told you we should have bailed." Then the next thing I know, the guy throws his arms around me and launches us high into the sky. My body sags for a moment when his paralyzing hold breaks, but as soon as I feel my freedom, I buck and thrash in his arms. His hold is like a steel vise.

"Let me go! You have no right," I yell at him, but he acts as though he can't feel my kicks and fists that pummel his arms and legs. What is with these people, grabbing me and carrying me off like I'm a child? No, more like a possession.

He ignores my commands as he flies over the treetops to the southeast, the wind whipping my hair in my face. Anger flares within me, and a burst of electricity explodes from my body. The power loosens the man's hold, and I twist out of his arms.

And plunge toward the ground in a free fall.

He swoops down to catch me, but with a thought, my own wings reappear. I try to bat them against the air while turning away from him, but I only manage to pitch myself into the top of a tree. The branches scrape across my legs. Unable to control the wings and take off in flight, I let myself glide to the ground, planning to run as soon as I land. But the gorgeous man alights in front of me and grabs my arm in another vise-like grip. Current shoots through me again, a pleasurable feeling that lights me up in ways it shouldn't. Not when I don't know this man.

"Stop," he orders when I try to free my arm from his grip. "I'm not going to hurt you. That's the last thing I'd do to you."

"Then let me go, or you'll *have* to hurt me because the only way I'm going with you is if I'm dead."

Another growl hums in his throat as he jerks me into him so that my chest presses against his hard one. His free hand grips my jaw, and he leans down and crushes his mouth to mine. His lips are persistent and demanding, and I can't help it at first, can't control the intense rush through my body, the electricity jolting pleasure through every nerve. My mouth opens for his automatically, my tongue unable to get enough of his tangy-sweet flavor, and my entire body molds into his as though it's always belonged here. My head goes woozy, and I'm about to completely lose myself in the kiss.

But then my wits return, and I'm horrified at my behavior. I shove my hands against his chest, pushing him away.

"What the hell do you think you're doing?" I jerk the back of my hand across my mouth, as though I could scrub away the tingles, wishing they didn't feel so amazing. "You just go around kissing strange women all the time?"

Agony flashes across his eyes, so intense, I almost feel bad, but he quickly recovers with a scowl. "I can't believe you don't remember that."

"You're telling me we've done that before?" How can I possibly not remember *that*? It must be the best kiss I've ever experienced in my life. How can I not remember *him*? He's the most beautiful creature I've ever seen. Not that I remember any faces or kisses from my past, but I can't imagine anything more beautiful on this earth. Any kiss more spine-tingling.

And since I don't remember what should have been unforgettable, he must be lying.

For a moment, he looks as though I've slapped him, but again, he quickly recovers. "First, we're getting you home and fixed up. And then, I'm going to kill that damn warlock protector of yours."

His hand darts out and grabs my wrist again, too fast for me to escape.

"Please don't," I beg, taking a different angle. I hope whatever he thinks he feels for me will soften his heart since my strength isn't enough to loosen his grip. "I won't tell anyone I saw you. And I'm no good as a hostage."

"Hostage?"

"You're trying to abduct me in exchange for something, right? For food? Weapons? Or maybe for my blood for that vampire?"

Or maybe for something else. Do Angels abduct girls for sex? Maybe he isn't an Angel. His wings aren't white. My wings aren't white, and I can almost guarantee I'm no Angel. And although he's inhumanly beautiful like an Angel, he's sexy in a sinful way. Maybe he's something else, and a certain part of me aches to know more.

"So you do know the vampires?"

I jolt back to reality. No. Knowing more about him is dangerous. This man is dangerous. He's too much for me. Too gorgeous, too frightening, too much for my mind and my body to handle. I need to get away from him before I do something stupid. Like kiss him again, because that one part of me really, really wants to.

"I know what they are, but I don't know them specifically." I try to yank my arm free, but damn, he's strong. "Please. Just let me go."

"Where?"

I hesitate. I don't know, but that's none of his business. "To my people. I'm pretty sure they're right over that ridge."

He lets out what might have been a snort, if beautiful Angel men snort. "We're your people. You don't know where you need to go because you have nowhere else, and somewhere in that head of yours, you know it."

Before I can answer, a screeching fills my head, like tires squealing on pavement, although I have no idea how I remember that sound. I flinch and wrap my free arm over my head as I squeeze my eyes shut.

"What's wrong?" the guy asks, and then his voice softens. "Something's in your head, isn't it?"

I don't know how he knows, but I nod as the sound dissipates.

"Can you hear my thoughts? Anyone's?"

My eyes pop open. "What the hell are you talking about?"

"Your telepathy. Is it working, or did you forget how to do that, too?" He blows out a harsh breath at the look on my face that must show my bewilderment. "Fucking great. Come on. I'm taking you home."

Before I can argue, another large shadow passes over us. He takes one look at the sky, pulls me close, and the world goes dark.

Only for a moment, though. The air whooshes out of my lungs, and when the light returns, I suck in big gulps of oxygen as I look around. We're no longer standing deep in the woods, but in front of a garage door flanked by concrete walls jutting out of the side of a hill.

"What the hell?" I'm unable to hide the wonder in my voice. "How'd we get here?"

The Angel's beautiful wings disappear, and at that thought, so do mine. His hand remains circled around my wrist, and ignoring my questions, he tugs me along as he strides for the tall, overhead door. Wings and the letters AK have been scratched into the paint of the metal surface of the door's frame, along with strange-looking symbols made of lines and swirls.

"I guess you can't give them a heads up we're here," he mumbles as he jabs his finger in a pattern over the symbols on one of the concrete walls. I don't understand what he means.

As the door begins to lift, Owen appears by our side. "Tristan, man, I'm sorry. I didn't think—"

The guy, Tristan, I figure, lifts his hand, and Owen's mouth snaps shut. "Obviously. Do you *ever* think, Scarecrow?"

"But I tried to stop her," Owen insists. "I honestly didn't think she drank any."

"Something *did* happen, though, didn't it?" Tristan bellows. "And *you* were supposed to protect her!"

Despite the anger in his voice and emanating off his body, Tristan gently pulls me forward to duck under the door. This is probably a stupid move, but I still can't pull free from his grip and have no choice but to follow. Besides, no instinctual voice screams at me to stop, and a part of me wants to go, the part that wishes this man would never release his hold on me.

"Get her to Carlie, make sure she's physically okay," Owen says. "I'll get Blossom. Surely we can figure out something."

"If you value your life, you better fucking hope so," Tristan barks at the same moment Owen disappears into thin air.

CHAPTER 3

Once we're inside, the door behind us closes, and panic rises within me as total darkness swallows us up. I wave my free hand in front of my face, and at first, I can't see, but then my eyes adjust although not the smallest glimmer of light intrudes. Where are we? What is this place? I have no concept of the size of where we are, although it feels rather small. Is this a cell? Have I made a huge mistake, trapping myself with an enemy? Or am I really supposed to be here? Who is this man to me? Is he really someone special? The look in his eyes—the pain when I didn't remember him—tells me yes, he is important to me. Or, at least, I'm important to him. Unless he's just a really good actor. Perhaps they all are, tricking me into believing I belong with them when I don't.

For some reason, though, this man makes me feel like I do. Maybe he's right and somewhere deep inside me, I know there's some kind of connection between us. That I'm meant to be here. Or maybe I'm stupidly smitten from that kiss, as much as I hate to admit it.

"There's nowhere for you to go. Can I trust you?" Tristan asks while letting go of my arm.

I feel more than see his shape move away, and a moment later, a line of light appears where I assume the floor to be. The sound of another door lifting fills the air. I stand in place as a large corridor, big enough to drive a truck through, opens up before me. A single overhead light casts a yellow glow, connected by wire to another far down the tunnel, and another beyond that. They're spaced far enough apart that dark shadows pool between them. The underground driveway stretches a good fifty yards away and downward until I can see no farther.

Tristan starts walking that way, leaving me behind. And talk about behind . . . he can't possibly be human. His ass certainly isn't. It belongs to a god.

"Come on." He no longer growls or barks. He sounds weary. Or maybe defeated is the better word, although with his power and poise, I doubt he knows defeat.

I glance over my shoulder, but only the garage door is there, and I see no way to open it so I can escape. I survey the ceiling and eye a vent twenty yards down, but I don't know where that leads. Otherwise, there are no other openings until way past Tristan.

After a moment of hesitation, I follow him, hoping I haven't walked into a trap. Of course, he hasn't taken my weapons, which doesn't seem like smart behavior when bringing someone into your safe place, so maybe this isn't their safe place after all. Or maybe he's stupid. No, that doesn't feel right. But I can't figure out why he hasn't disarmed me.

He turns around, walking backwards, and his eyes fall on my hand still gripping my dagger.

"I can't confiscate *all* of your weapons," he says, "so I have no choice but to trust you. Don't make me regret it."

He returns to walking forward. I keep my hand on the hilt, just in case, but slip the blade into the sheath at my hip. At this point, I really have no choice, either, but to trust him. I don't know what he means about not being able to take all of my weapons, but he doesn't seem too worried about them, whatever they are. Probably because he has that debilitating power to paralyze me. All bets are off when he does that. I don't ever want to feel so helpless again.

We follow the corridor downward, rounding a couple of bends, and pass by a space that opens up large enough for two or three trucks to park side by side. Adjacent to it is a closed off area with *Intake* written on its door. Tristan looks over his shoulder at me.

"That's your office." He indicates the door while studying my face, as though waiting for some sign of recognition from me. I glance at the door, but feel no sense of familiarity.

"So you're putting me to work?" I ask. "You don't know my skill set. I don't even know what I can do."

He sighs and continues on. "Guess we'll figure that out later. Come on."

We come to a junction where what I guess to be a map is embossed into the limestone wall. I assume the upside-down egg shape, with its lines and numbers, depict this shelter and its hallways, with a little dot between the numbers 103 and 104. I glance up and spy a numbered sign hanging from the ceiling to my right that shows 104.

We turn that way, passing rows and rows of industrial-type shelving stocked with various supplies, from toilet paper and hand sanitizer to buckets, boxes of cans, and bags labelled RICE, FLOUR, MEATS, and various other food. Many of the shelves are sparse, though, and we pass many empty rows, except for one shelf that holds several cases of bottled water.

"Storage area." Tristan points down a corridor. "Conversions."

He looks at me with more expectation in his eyes. I fail to meet it again. We walk silently except for the sound of our feet hitting the stone floor and the distant murmurs of people talking. He apparently gives up on getting anything out of me. We make two more turns and come to what appears to be a building within the shelter, with concrete block walls stacked to the ceiling. He takes me through a door in the wall marked *Medical*. My brow furrows. This isn't the first place I've expected him to take me. *Holding Cells* or *Torture Rooms* is more like it.

The smells of the place have changed during our trek, from a somewhat damp, musky odor near the doors to the slight tang of recycled and conditioned air the farther down we came. Here, the sharp bite of bleach hits my nose, with underlying threads of fragranced hand sanitizer, sour vomit, and metallic blood.

"Carlie," Tristan barks from the reception area, and a blond woman, in her late twenties, maybe, rounds a corner. She wears regular clothes—a white t-shirt and faded blue jeans—and a stethoscope hangs around her neck.

Her blue eyes survey each of us, as though assessing us. Of course, she doesn't find any injuries. "Can it wait? I'm trying to put an IV into Saundra. She's dehydrated and becoming pretty ill."

Tristan throws a look at me. "Hurry. Something's wrong with Alexis."

Carlie's eyes bounce to me again, confusion filling her face. "Um, okay. Take her to two. I'll be there as soon as I can."

19

"Make it faster," Tristan orders as she disappears back around the corner from where she'd come. "Come on."

"I don't need medical attention," I say. "I'm not hurt."

"The hell you aren't." His large hand circles my wrist, and he tugs me as he turns to our right.

We come to a door marked 2 and enter what looks like a makeshift medical exam room. How can I remember what a stethoscope is or what an exam room looks like but not my own name? The table is in rough shape, appearing as though it's been salvaged from ruins, not purchased from a supply company. Rather than the normal cabinets and sink, there's a wooden dresser with a plastic bucket, a container of hand sanitizer, and other supplies in a neat row on the top of it.

Tristan nods toward the exam table, gesturing for me to sit on it, while he leans against the wall, lifts one leg to brace his foot against it, and crosses his thickly muscled arms over his broad chest. I don't jump up on the table, as he apparently wants me to do, but lean against it and mimic his pose. Neither of us utters a word. I'm full of questions, but I already know he's not so full of answers. I scowl at the floor, but can't help stealing several glances his way. Yep. He's too damn hot for my own good.

A quick rap on the door is followed by Carlie entering. Her eyes survey me again. "What's going on?"

"Nothing. I'm fine," I say.

"You look fine."

"Ask her her mother's name," Tristan says.

Carlie looks at me expectantly. I try to search my uncooperative brain, but there's nothing. I say the only name I can think of.

"Elli. She's in a camp back near that lake, waiting for me."

Carlie frowns as she studies me, then looks at Tristan.

"She remembers nothing about her life," he says.

Carlie's frown deepens, then she orders me, "Up on the table."

"I said I'm fine," I protest without moving.

With a sigh, she pulls a small flashlight out of her pocket and shines it in my eyes without waiting for me to mount the table.

"How many fingers?" She holds up three, and I tell her so.

She holds up more fingers to each side of my head and asks again. I give her the correct answers. She pockets the flashlight and lifts her hands toward my head, and I flinch away.

"I need to check for bumps," she explains. "You don't seem to have a concussion, but I need to make sure you don't have a head injury."

"Owen thinks it's black magic," Tristan says. "Probably from the water. Not an injury."

"She drank the water before it was tested?" Disbelief colors Carlie's tone.

"Owen supposedly tried to stop her, but she must have. She's not right."

"I don't feel any injuries," she says as she massages my head. She looks into my eyes. "You don't remember anything? Who I am?"

"Carlie," I say.

"She already heard me say it," Tristan reminds her.

Carlie steps back and studies me, one arm across her chest, holding her elbow as her other hand grips her chin. "I don't know what to do with black magic. Sounds like you need a mage, not me."

"Owen's getting Blossom," Tristan says. "I just want you to make sure there's nothing physically wrong with my wife."

"I'm really limited in what tests I can do, but . . ." Carlie goes on, but I tune her out, stuck on what Tristan had said.

Specifically, on the words "my wife." He has to be joking. I'm married? To *him*? How could I not remember *that*? Although, it at least explains his forwardness in kissing me like he had. But still. This can't be happening.

". . . bring Elli and Brie here."

Tristan's speaking, but I hadn't heard the words until now. The name Elli catches my attention, since it'd been the first name to pop into my mind only moments ago. There's an actual Elli here. Is that the reason I'd thought of that name first? If so, then these people haven't been lying to me. Not completely, anyway. I must come from here. If only I could remember.

Carlie leaves the room. Tristan doesn't so much as budge.

"Are Elli and Brie the leaders of this place?" If I did belong here, there must be a reason I'd blurted Elli as my mother's name. Whether she's my actual mother or has taken on a motherly role here in the bunker, I don't know.

One corner of Tristan's mouth tilts up in a half-smile. "In a way."

A few minutes later, I hear crying in the distance. A baby's cry. And . . . Holy shit! My breasts suddenly grow hot and hard, becoming tight and painful. My shoulders hunch over, and I cross my arms over my boobs. I discreetly try to press my hands against them to massage them. They're as hard and heavy as concrete, my skin stretching tightly over them. And dear God, do they *hurt*. As the crying moves closer, the pressure in my chest builds until I think my breasts might explode. Then . . . a sticky wetness fills my top. My eyes grow in horror. What in the actual *fuck*?

They did explode!

Tristan's nose twitches, then his half-smile grows into a full one as he looks at me. "Are you leaking?"

"Leaking? Leaking *what*?"

The feeling becomes so gross, I have to turn away from him and look down my top.

"What. The. Hell?" I yell. Both the bra and the tank top I wear are soaked through, and my breasts swim in a white liquid. "I'm not leaking. I'm gushing!"

The man behind me chuckles, and I almost spin on him to let him have it, but I'm too confused by the state of my boobs. I pull the fabric away from my skin, and more white liquid streams from my nipples. The door opens, and the cries come clear and near—right behind me. My boobs become full-on geysers.

"I think they're hungry," Carlie says from behind me.

Oh no. Hell no. This can not be happening.

I look over my shoulder to find Carlie and a young woman with dark hair and blue eyes, each holding a crying baby. Carlie holds her baby out to me. I spin and back into the corner, shaking my head vehemently while holding my arm across my boobs. Pressing against the nipples seems to slow the flow.

"No way," I whisper as I stare at them in horror. "Don't tell me I'm a nursemaid! Where are Elli and Brie? I thought you were bringing them here. I want to talk to them now. And I want the fuck out of here!"

"Look at them, Alexis," Tristan says. "Really look at them."

I peer at the babies, and something nudges me in the heart. My mind doesn't know what I'm supposed to be looking at, but my heart tugs toward them.

"They're adorable, even crying," I say. "But what am I supposed to see?"

"This *is* Elli and Brie," Carlie answers.

I shake my head and look at Tristan. "I thought you said they were your leaders."

He studies me for a long moment, then releases a heavy sigh. "Teah, get them some bottles. Carlie, can you get the pump?"

The women both nod and leave with the crying infants.

"*You're* our leader, Lex," Tristan says once they're gone, his voice low and heavy. "Elli and Brie . . . Elliana and Brielle? They're our daughters. Yours and mine."

My breath catches. My eyes hurt, they bug so much.

"No," I whisper. I shake my head again. "Impossible. Don't you think I would know that I'm a mom? Don't you think I would know my own *babies*? My *husband*?"

He watches me, and the agony returns to his eyes, this time not fleeting, but lasting. His voice comes out so heavy and so full of pain, my own heart hurts. "Yeah, Lex, I'd thought you would."

CHAPTER 4

*C*arlie enters the room at that moment. I blink back the tears threatening at the corners of my eyes, although I'm not sure why I want to cry. It's almost as if I actually feel the man's emotional pain in my own heart, even in my soul. I don't know what to do or say to make it go away.

"What is that?" I ask instead, gesturing at the items in Carlie's hands: a small machine, two tubes, two bottles, and a plastic cone attached to each bottle.

"A breast pump." Tristan holds out his hands to take the pieces, but Carlie doesn't turn them over to him. "You have to pump to keep the supply going."

"*What?*" I demand as I cross my other arm over my breasts.

"Maybe I should help her." Carlie's tone makes it sound as though it's more than an offer—more like a very strong suggestion.

Tristan eyes me, runs his hand over the back of his head, and walks out of the room without a word.

I cringe when the door slams shut. "He hates me, and I can't do anything about it."

"Trust me, the man can never in his wildest dreams hate you. He has more love for you than . . ." She drifts off and lets out a sigh. "Let's just say every woman dreams to have a man love her half as much as Tristan loves you."

My lungs shudder as I inhale. "Why don't I remember that? Shouldn't I remember something so huge?"

"I don't know, hun, but we'll figure it out." She sets the items in her arms on the dresser and begins to assemble the pieces. "You'll need to take off your shirt."

"Gladly." I grab the hem and yank the wet tank over my head, taking the bra with it. My boobs fall free, spraying milk everywhere. I quickly cover them with my hands, not out of modesty but to control the mess. Carlie stares at me with wide eyes. "What?"

"You're, uh, not usually so . . . showy."

"Oh." I shrug. "The top was soaked. It was gross."

Her gaze bounces down for a second before coming back up to my face, her skin flushed. I can't blame her—I'd noticed my great boobs earlier. But then I see what she's more likely looking at. An ugly scar of puckered skin stretches from my right shoulder to my sternum, cutting across the top of my breast. I wonder where it came from, but as soon as I release a hand to touch it, I quickly forget about it when the milk sprays again. Carlie approaches me with the contraption in hand.

"I know this is really awkward," she says, "but it *will* make you feel better."

Awkward doesn't begin to describe the situation as she attaches the bottles to my breasts. And oh my God is the sensation weird when she turns the machine on, like a vacuum trying to suck my entire boob up. I watch with a mixture of horror and fascination as the milk begins filling the bottles, and I envision a dairy cow hooked up to a milking machine. That's exactly how I feel, too—like a freaking milk cow!

Within a few minutes, though, the promised relief comes. I actually moan out loud as the ache and swelling drain away, my eyes drifting closed with the reprieve. When I open them, Carlie's staring at my left boob. My eyebrows spring up, and her gaze flies sideways when she realizes she's caught. Again.

"Uh, sorry." She chuckles. "It's just . . . your chest is so interesting."

Her eyes drift down again, and I follow her gaze to my left breast. No scar on this one. Rather, swirls and arcs, darker in pigment and slightly raised, mark my skin over my heart. The stylized design looks almost like it could be a sword or dagger with wings. Embedded in the center, as though pressed into my flesh, is a stone, perhaps a ruby or a red garnet. I finger the stone, and a warm flush runs through me as the image of Tristan's face pops into my mind. Something in my heart or soul stirs, making me gasp. As soon as I drop my hand, the feeling dissipates, but the heat doesn't.

"I think I'll go get something to clean you up and some fresh clothes." Carlie hurries out of the room, probably thinking the flush came from embarrassment. I don't know what any of it means, though, so I have no reason to be ashamed.

She returns at about the same time both bottles are nearly filled, and my breasts are beginning to hurt from the suction. She takes the bottles and hands me a washcloth and a bottle of water, half full.

"Sorry, but this is all we have," she says. "Our water supply is about tapped. That's why you were at the lake—looking for a new source. We only have a small amount left for everyone. I'll leave your top right here and let you clean up."

Carlie leaves once more, and I do my best in washing the sticky milk off of me and then pick up the bra she'd brought. With a body like this— and a man like Tristan to appreciate it—I feel like I should be wearing sexy lace and silk, but instead the bra's plain white cotton with an underwire. Each cup has a flap that can be pulled down, presumably for nursing. I sigh. Is this really mine? Is this really my life? When I put it on, it fits perfectly. So does the T-shirt and leggings she'd brought me.

The evidence that this is, indeed, my life is piling up to the point I can no longer deny it. As Tristan had said, some part of me must know they've been telling me the truth all along. So why can't I remember any of this? What really happened to me? Was it really something in the water? If we were there to test it, why would I have been so stupid as to drink it? Huh. *Am* I stupid?

When Carlie returns, she draws some of my blood into a tube, and then has me pee in a cup. She also makes me lie down on the exam table and then prods around from my neck to my pelvis. Finally, not finding anything obvious, she leads me out of the Medical building.

"I'll show you to the kitchen. Blossom should be there. She'll be of more help than I am. I hope."

"They keep saying Blossom and Owen should be able to help me," I say as I follow Carlie. "Why them and not you? You're a doctor, right? Or not?"

"Yes, I am, but nothing is medically wrong with you that I can tell. I'll test the blood and urine as best as I can with what I have, and I'll let you know if I find anything indicating internal bleeding, low cell counts, or the like, but I think you're right. You're physically fine. I wish I could do a brain scan, but we don't have the equipment."

"So what are Owen and Blossom—is that really her name?"

Carlie smiles at me as we approach another "building" of cinder blocks inside the cavern. "Yeah, it is. She's your best friend. Besides Tristan, anyway. And maybe Owen and Vanessa. You're close with all of them."

I sigh. "And I remember none of them."

"You will." She opens a swinging door and holds it for me. "We'll get you all sorted out. We have to. We need you."

The fragrance of freshly baked bread immediately makes my mouth water, and my stomach growls with all of the smells of food cooking.

"Low water supplies means no soup tonight." Carlie's voice lifts a notch as we cross the large kitchen to the industrial-sized sinks lining a part of one wall. "I'm kind of glad, to be honest. Soup stretches out our supplies so they'll last longer, but we have it almost every day. It gets old, no matter how good they are at coming up with new varieties."

She demonstrates how to wash the breast pump paraphernalia since, apparently, I'll be doing this a lot, then shows me the refrigerator where they store the milk. Several bottles line the shelf, in addition to the two we slide in, placing them at the back.

"You'll have to pump frequently to keep your supply up. Otherwise, you'll go dry and then those babies will be in trouble. And that means staying hydrated and fed. Don't you worry about taking more than your share of water. Everyone understands. But if we don't get the water issue fixed soon . . ." Carlie trails off, the concern weighing heavily in her voice. The water situation here seems to be dire.

"How did this happen?" I ask, but then I realize if I'm the leader, the water situation is my fault. I must not be a good leader. Maybe I *am* stupid.

"Hey, Alexis," a soft voice says from behind me.

Carlie and I both turn to find a thin woman with blond hair, big hazel eyes, and breasts that put mine to shame. She frowns when I don't respond. "Um, Blossom? That's my name. I'm a witch. We're really good friends. I mean, I consider you my bestie, besides Jax, of course, but you have a lot of besties, so, um, anyway . . ." She glances at Carlie, who provides no help, but instead excuses herself to return to her patients. Blossom gives me a smile that I can tell is forced. "Come with me. Your council will gather later so we can figure out what to do. I'm sure Owen

27

and I will get you fixed in no time, but for now, there are other problems, too. Owen's out in the dining room. I'll have someone bring you out a plate of food. I'm sure you're starving."

The woman goes on and on, and I wonder if her witchiness gives her some way to not have to breathe. Her witchiness . . . I seem to accept that as easily as I'd known about the vampires. But somewhere deep inside, I feel like I haven't always known about these creatures. That they haven't always been so out in the open with the Normans. Wait . . .

"What are Normans?" I blurt.

"Normal humans," Blossom says. "That's what we, the supernaturals, call the normal people. That or norms. You remember that?"

"Yeah, I guess I do."

"But nothing else?"

"Some stuff. But apparently, not the important things."

We go through a different swinging door than Carlie and I had come into, exiting the kitchen into a vast area full of an eclectic collection of tables and chairs. Some are small, for two or four people, with mismatched wooden and plastic chairs, while others are cafeteria-style, long enough to seat a couple dozen on their benches. Vases of various sizes, shapes, and colors, holding plastic and fabric flowers, have been placed on many of the tables, a small gesture to brighten up the atmosphere. Owen sits at a square table for four, and Blossom drops down next to him. The only reason I join them is because someone follows right behind us with what smells like a grilled cheese sandwich, and my stomach rumbles.

"Are you claiming us yet?" Owen asks after I've devoured several bites. He's finished his food and has been watching me with those deep blue eyes of his.

"I don't think I can deny that I'm supposed to be here anymore," I admit before taking another bite. When I finish chewing, I add, "But I don't claim anything yet."

"Blossom, you'll need to pass off your kitchen duties to someone else," Owen says. "Fixing our matriarch ranks up at top priority."

"Agreed." Blossom bobs her head. "Already done. I just wish I had all of my books, but I'd left them at home, so they probably don't even exist anymore. The experimenting should be fun, though. As long as, you know, we don't make her any worse."

My eyebrows shoot up, and my voice rises an octave. "What kind of experimenting are you going to do on me? Wait—with *magic?*"

"Don't worry," Owen says. "Not on you."

"We'll have to run a bunch of tests on the water," Blossom clarifies. "Try to figure out what specific kind of magic is in it to cause the amnesia. Hopefully, all that time Owen spent with Kali learning alchemy will come in handy."

Owen frowns, but nods. "As much as we hate her, she knew her potions. I already have a couple of ideas to try."

He pushes back his chair and stands, then gestures for me to do the same. I cock my head as I hold up what remains of my sandwich.

"Can I finish eating?" I ask.

"Sure. I need to do a quick assessment, then you can do whatever you want. Just stand up for a minute."

I eye him skeptically.

"He's our most powerful warlock," Blossom says. "And your protector. He won't do anything to hurt you."

Heh. Tristan doesn't seem to think so. Tristan doesn't seem to be impressed at all with Owen's abilities, especially as my protector. I, however, don't really know anything. I feel like a lost child in a grown-up's body—one that apparently serves up milk like a soda fountain. So I stand, put my arms out as Owen requested, and let him do some kind of magical scan.

"Meet me in the lab in ten," he says to Blossom before rushing away.

"Sure thing." She observes me as I take the last few bites of my meal. "I guess you need to be shown to your quarters, huh? You don't remember where they are?"

I shake my head. "And soon. I need to use the bathroom."

We put my dishes in the bin for washing, then Blossom leads me to the communal bathroom and gives me directions to my living quarters from there. I'm relieved to know I'd be left alone for a while, because I really need some space. Some quiet time to figure out what's going on. Maybe to find myself again.

I pause at the bathroom mirror over the sink, surprised at my reflection. Big, brown eyes, hair the color of a dark penny, smooth skin with an olive tone—my features don't startle me as much as my overall appearance. I hadn't expected to be so pretty, even without a trace of makeup, and I look so young, especially considering I have babies. *And* I'm supposedly the matriarch of this place. Whatever that is, it makes me sound old, but I appear to be younger than everyone I've met so far.

Maybe they have been lying to me, after all. Feeding me bullshit lines they think will keep me here and make me more cooperative.

Someone enters the communal bathroom, and I straighten up to find Sheree, a slight limp in her gait I hadn't noticed before. Her face fills with hesitation as she steps around me. When she comes out of the bathroom stall, I still haven't moved.

"Are you okay?" she asks, concern filling her dark eyes.

I shrug. "I guess so. I really don't know that, either, though."

"I'm so sorry this happened."

"It's not your fault . . . is it?"

She frowns. "I'm not as fast as I used to be on two legs. Otherwise, I would have been there sooner. I really thought Owen stopped you in time, though."

I don't know what to say to that, so I return to studying my reflection. "How old am I?"

Through the mirror, I watch her brows pinch together for a moment while she pumps a blob of hand sanitizer into her palm. "Twenty-nine? I think. Maybe thirty. In Norman years, anyway."

I look at her reflection. "What does that mean?"

"Well, when you went through the *Ang'dora*, you aged backward. They say you went back to when you were nineteen, when you were mentally, physically, and emotionally strongest. That was three years ago, so I guess you're more like twenty-two mentally, but you don't physically age."

I turn around and blink at her. "The *Ang'dora*?"

She pulls a funny face. "I'm a Were, a shifter. I'm tiger and human, much simpler than you. I can't explain the *Ang'dora* as well as Tristan could, but it was a big change you went through. All of your kind do. Well, did. Now that you're Earth's Angels, I don't know if your daughters still will. That was when you received all of your gifts from the Angels. It's when I first met you, when you were going through the *Ang'dora*."

"What kinds of gifts?"

"The telepathy, the electrical power, Amadis power, strength, speed, heightened senses . . . all kinds of gifts. You have all the best qualities of vampires and shifters without being either, as well as certain forms of magic. Now, you're even *more* than all that. You and Tristan said the ascended matriarchs called you an Earth's Angel. He's one, too, and so are Elliana and Brielle. And all the Ames brothers."

I stare at her, at a loss for words. She smiles at what must be the disbelief on my face.

"Honestly, Tristan can tell you more than I can. It's a long story. But maybe you'll just get your memory back. We all kind of need that."

I nod as I follow her out the door. This life that is supposedly mine is totally baffling.

Sheree heads for the kitchen while I follow Blossom's directions to my room. Maybe the familiarity there will help me remember. And if not, maybe some time by myself will help me process everything and pull forth those memories. I nearly break into a run as I hurry past the rows of residences that fill several sections, anxious to be alone. When I reach Section 608, which is mine, according to Blossom, I turn and almost fly up the middle flight of wooden steps to the second floor.

When I open the door, though, I freeze. How can I be so dumb to think I'd be alone?

CHAPTER 5

*T*ristan sits on a large area rug covering a wooden floor, next to a queen-size mattress and box spring set that has no frame. He huddles over one of the babies, changing her diaper. The other baby lies on a cushion next to him, a small, white puppy curled at her feet. The baby's little head turns toward me when I walk in, and her hands wave in the air, as though she recognizes me. How sad that she knows me, but I don't know her.

Again, my heart feels a tug toward her and her twin. Toward this whole scene before me. I don't know if it's because something deep within remembers this is my family, or simply because it's an endearing scene. In fact, watching this muscular man, whom I know holds great power in one finger, being so gentle and sweet with the tiny human in front of him, makes everything inside me go soft. When he picks her up and nuzzles his face into her neck, my heart melts into goo.

But it also twists and aches, and I have to blink against the pricks in my eyes.

I turn back to leave.

"You should stay." Tristan's voice comes low and soft.

I pause. "I'm sorry. I didn't mean to intrude."

"Lex, this is your home. You're not intruding. Please, stay."

Reluctantly, I turn around to face him, although I stand back, up against the door, my hands twisting around each other. He still sits on the floor, holding the baby in one arm. I glance over at the bed. "I, uh, just wanted to lie down. Try to think things through."

He picks up the other baby with his free hand and stands. "We'll go then."

My hand flies up, and I shake my head. "Oh, no. I'm not going to run them out of their own home."

"I can leave them with you," he suggests, and I don't know whether I'm horrified or excited about that idea. I think a little bit of both.

"I'm not going to run you out, either."

"Look, I'll take them for a walk. You lie down with Sasha and get some rest. Maybe regenerating will do you some good. We'll, uh, figure out the living arrangements later."

Before I can answer, he crosses the room in two long strides. I sidestep away. His finger twitches, and the door opens on its own, and at the same moment, the walkie-talkie hanging on his belt loop squawks.

"Moose, we got a problem. Over." Owen's voice comes through the device.

Tristan twists, as though trying to figure out how to grab the thing while holding two babies. He looks at me for help, but I'm not about to take it off his pants. I can't trust my body with that kind of closeness. He begins to shift one of the babies to hold both in his left arm, but my hands lift on their own accord to take her. And next thing I know, I'm staring into warm, brown eyes almost exactly like the ones I'd been inspecting in the mirror.

The walkie-talkie squawks again, and Tristan grabs it. "Is this about Alexis? Over."

"No. It's about sick bay. Over."

Tristan chuckles. "This isn't a spaceship, Scarecrow, remember? You mean the medical unit? Over."

"It's not a military base, either," Owen retorts. "Whatever you want to call it, Carlie's getting swamped with patients. Severe dehydration, apparently, and we're about out of bottled water. We need to turn the pumps back on."

"We'll drain the source in days," Tristan says.

"I know, but we need to do *something*, dude."

Tristan swears under his breath, though I have no problem hearing it along with a another string of profanities. He looks at me and hesitates for a moment as our eyes lock, then he pushes the button to the communicator. "I'll meet you there. Over and out."

"Ten-four."

Tristan glances at the bundle in his arm and the one in mine, and then his eyes return to my face. "I'd ask Teah or Teal, their usual babysitters, but they're teaching right now. This is normally our time with the babies. And I can't exactly take them near the sick, in case it's more than dehydration."

My stomach flutters at the thought of taking care of these helpless little creatures by myself, but his beautiful, expressive eyes render me speechless with their pleas.

"They're fed and changed and will be ready for a nap any time now," he continues, and when I glance down at the one in my arms, her eyelids are already drooping.

I swallow, then nod, before reaching out for the one he holds. He explains how to tell Brielle from Elliana—"We put Brie in the warm colors and Elli in the cool shades"—and shows me where their diapers and clothes are stored. "Just in case," he says.

"I'm sure they'll sleep the whole time I'm gone," Tristan promises as the walkie-talkie screeches again. "I'll be back as soon as I can. Thank you."

He's thanking me for taking care of my own children. I give him a weak smile. "Of course. I'm their mother, right?"

He returns my smile with a small one, then hurries off. I think I hear him mutter something about my motherly instincts jogging my memory, although it's more like I think the idea in my head but with his voice.

"Wait," I call to him. "Who's Sasha?"

"The lykora," he says.

Lykora? I wonder to myself.

He turns the corner, but I still hear when he adds, "The dog."

I use my shoulder to shut the door, and as I turn back toward the room, I look down at the babies in my arms and try not to freak out. They've both drifted off already. I hope that means I can get some rest, too. I lean over the single baby bed next to the mattress—since there's only one, they must share it, as small as they are—and I can't help it. I snuggle against each one's cheek and give them a kiss before putting them down. They smell so sweet, and their skin feels like velvet.

My heart grows about five times its previous size.

I hunt around the room for something personal that belongs to this Alexis, but the twelve-by-twenty-foot room doesn't contain much to tell me anything. The queen-sized bed, the baby bed, a bookshelf full of baby items, a rocking chair, a baby swing, and a dresser furnish the place. A lamp sits on top of the bookshelf, and white Christmas lights are strung in a zigzag pattern overhead. A rod with a few items of clothing hanging on it dangles from the ceiling in the corner. There are no books, although I don't know if books have survived the world's destruction. I imagine a mother to these twins and leader of this place doesn't have much time for reading, anyway.

When I lie down, the side of the bed closest to the baby bed smells faintly of dark chocolate and raspberries. I roll over to the other side, and Tristan's scent envelops me—the tangy-sweetness of mangos, papayas, lime, sage, and a hint of man. The fragrance makes my mouth water and my lower regions warm. I roll back over to the other, safer side, and try to ignore the tears welling in my eyes as I wonder how I can name those scents—foods that as far as I know don't exist anymore and I hadn't smelled in ages—but can't recall what I did yesterday.

Sasha jumps on the bed and settles on her haunches in front of me while seeming to study my face for a moment. She's small enough to fit in my hands, all white with big black eyes that seem to hold entirely too much wisdom for a little dog. With a snuff of approval, she lies down, curling up next to me. I dig my fingers into her thick, soft fur, and the scent of baby powder rises. I let her steady breathing settle my own.

Sleep brings dreams. Terrible nightmares of real Angels, with white, pearlescent wings, fiercely fighting Demons with horned heads, mottled skin, and tails. They fight with ancient weapons, such as swords and maces, and the clanging rattles in my ears. Below them, on the snow-covered ground, another battle wages, and I recognize faces I'd met today—a winged Tristan, Vanessa, Owen, Blossom, and others whose names I don't know. Then suddenly, the fighting stops, and a deathly silence falls. An un-winged Tristan stands in front of me, but he disappears, along with the people he and the others had been fighting. Except, he also stands next to me, with wings again, and I realize they are not the same person.

"Dorian will be okay," Tristan murmurs.

The piercing sound of screaming babies jerks me out of sleep.

My breasts are rock solid again, aching with pressure and the heavy strain against my skin. But I push the pain aside to focus on the babies. I pick them both up, but that doesn't seem to help. I lay them down on the cushion and grab diapers and wipes off the nearby shelf, but when I check their diapers, they're clean. When my boobs spring leaks again, I can't ignore what I'd known all along.

"Oh, crap."

I look around frantically for bottles. Do they not have a fridge up here, at least a mini one? Well, of course not. She—I—would have fed them directly. The thought of them on my boobs, though, freaks me out. I don't even know how to do it!

I gather the crying girls in my arms and stride for the door. I'll take them to the kitchen to retrieve their bottles and the pump, except I can't figure out how to open the door while holding both babies. *Could use an extra hand here!* I mentally scream with frustration. At the moment I wonder if I have the same power as Tristan to open the door without touching the knob, it bursts open.

"Are you okay?" He swoops in and takes a baby from me.

Several others stand at the door. Blossom rushes in, too, and takes the other twin.

"They're, uh, hungry," I say, momentarily surprised by the response, as though they're at my beck and call. Or at the babies', anyway. Now that my arms are free, I cross my arms and subtly press my fists against my aching boobs. "And I guess I need the pump."

"On it." Blossom swishes her free hand in a flourish. A moment later, full bottles, empty bottles, and the pump soar through the air and into the room. She smiles at my wide-eyed expression. "I'm getting pretty good at summoning things, yeah? Owen's teaching me."

Everyone but Tristan leaves us, and Blossom closes the door behind her. He sits on the bed and props the babies on pillows, then teases their lips with the bottles' nipples. They balk at first, refusing to take them as they continue crying, but Tristan speaks soothingly to them until they finally give in to their hunger. Guilt tugs at my heart strings—they want the real thing. I can't bring myself to do that, though. I don't even know how. Once they quiet, Tristan looks up at me.

I still stand in the middle of the room, holding the pump equipment and staring at their perfection. Until his stunning yet piercing gaze gets to me.

I clear my throat and hold up the pump. "Um, where can I go to do this?"

Confusion flickers in his eyes, and then he lifts a finger from one of the bottles and draws a line in the air with it. The rocking chair next to me spins around to face the corner, making me jump.

"I don't think what people have is contagious, but I'd rather not risk taking the babies out there," he says.

I shake my head. "No, of course not."

"Don't worry. I won't watch." He returns his doting attention to his daughters. If this man loves his wife half as much as he obviously loves his daughters, she's one lucky lady. "But you can use a blanket, if you prefer."

I sit in the chair with my back to them, assemble everything as Carlie had shown me, and then relief comes. I can't help the sigh. I settle back to let the machine do its thing and close my eyes. As I begin to relax, the last image of my dream returns.

"Who's Dorian?" I ask.

Tristan had been baby-talking with the twins, but he suddenly falls silent. He doesn't answer at first, and in the quiet, I realize the pump's sound has changed. I turn it off and remove the bottles, setting them on the nearby shelf.

"Do you remember him?" Tristan finally asks, hope filling his voice.

"Not exactly. I had a dream."

He falls quiet again. After making sure I'm covered, I turn the chair around using my legs. I watch him expectantly. He stares at the girls, whose mouths sucking on the nearly empty bottles make the only sound. He finally looks up at me, and his eyes are sad again.

I tilt my head. "What's wrong? Was . . . was he your brother?"

His mouth twitches, and a low, dark chuckle rumbles in his throat. "No. He's our son."

My jaw drops, my mouth hanging wide open. Another child I don't remember? How?

"We have a son, too? That old?"

Tristan sighs. "It's a long story."

I echo his sigh. "Everything seems to be a long story here."

"Yeah." He nods. "It is. You started to write it once. Our story."

"Really?"

"You were a famous author, in the Before time. One of the most successful ever. Your books helped a lot of people. But our story . . . I think you wrote it to work through everything, not for anyone else's eyes. You filled up a hundred or so notebooks, the equivalent of several full-length novels, before everything got really bad. They were never published, of course. You put them in the Sacred Archives, so who knows what happened to them. Maybe the Angels have them."

"Sacred Archives?"

Tristan shrugs. "Only Amadis daughters knew exactly what it was."

"Was?" I pick up on the use of past tense.

"It was part of the matriarch's mansion, which has been destroyed, along with everything else."

"Oh. Of course." I nod and frown at the same time. "I can't believe I don't remember any of this."

"Hopefully, you will soon. Although, some parts I wish you wouldn't have to."

"Like what happened to our son? It's bad, isn't it?" The lingering feeling from the dream feels too strong to not be real.

The babies finish eating, and he puts the empty bottles to the side. He picks up one, Brielle, based on her yellow onesie, and hands her to me. He places a cloth over my shoulder, then shows me how to burp her. He lays Elliana against his own shoulder and begins patting and rubbing her back, his hand like a giant's compared to her tiny body.

"Dorian," he finally says, "is doing what he needs to do. He's with the Demon's army."

My hand pauses in midair. "Our *son* is with the *Demons' army?*"

His only answer comes as a nod.

Oh my god. I shake my head as I return to patting the baby's back. This is too much, too difficult to believe. "What kind of woman gives her blessing to her son defecting to the evil side? What kind of leader does such a thing?"

"You didn't exactly give your blessing. You've always vowed to get him back. But you've come to accept that he is doing what needs to be done right now." Elliana squirms, and he sits her on his leg, letting her lean into his palm. Her chin rests on the curve of his thumb and forefinger as he pats her back with his other hand. "You're a good mom, Lex. And a good leader. And you'll be even better now, as soon as we get your memory restored."

I have a hard time believing that. Not from what I've seen and heard already. Maybe everyone would be better off if I never do remember and someone else takes over as leader. Tristan seems to be a good candidate.

Brielle lets out a belch so big, I'm astonished her little body can hold that much air. I can't help but laugh, and then Elliana mimics her twin.

Tristan and I both laugh as the babies coo contentedly. A moment later, they both begin to squirm and a distinctive stink hits my nose.

"Not too long ago, you were teaching me all of this," Tristan says as he demonstrates how to change their diapers and what to do with the dirty ones.

"How old are they, anyway?"

"They'll be six months in a couple of weeks." He snickers. "You'd normally be able to tell us exactly how many weeks and days old they are."

I give him a teasing smile. "And you can't?"

A small return grin plays on his mouth, but he doesn't admit to the obsession.

With the girls cleaned up and happy, we sit on the floor and let them play.

Tristan clears his throat. "So your telepathy's back. That's a good sign."

My eyes cut sideways at him. "My . . . *telepathy?*"

He twists his head to return my stare. "You used it to call for help with the girls. We all heard you. In our heads."

CHAPTER 6

"*Y*ou're saying you can hear my thoughts?" I ask in disbelief, quickly followed by a panicked, "Can you hear them *now*?"

They'd mentioned telepathy before, but I'd paid it no attention. I'd thought I'd heard the word wrong or had misunderstood what they meant by it.

"Yes and no," Tristan replies. "Only when you want me to."

"Obviously not." I stand and walk across the room then back again, anxious energy filling me.

"Well, when you were new to it, you sometimes lost control. You probably don't have much control now, since you don't remember you even have the gift."

Oh great. That's comforting. I huff out a breath. He probably heard that thought, too. If so, he doesn't acknowledge it. And what kind of *gift* is this?

Another thought sends my heart racing again. "Do you have it, too? Does everybody here?"

Who's been listening to me all this time?

He shakes his head. "Only you. It's a powerful ability the Angels reserve for a select few. Those who can handle it without abusing it."

I let this sink in as I pace back and forth in the small space. "So I can send out thoughts? Like mind-talk?"

"Yes. And you can receive them, too."

"I can hear other people's thoughts? As in go into their heads and listen to them?" This is insane.

"Yes. That's why it's such a rare gift. In the wrong kind of person—in most people, really—the ability to listen to other people's thoughts about anything and everything, whenever they want to . . . you can imagine the temptation. The power can be easily abused."

I push my hands through my hair and dig my fingertips into my scalp, as though I can reach into my mind and remove anyone's thoughts—or the entire telepathic ability. I can't imagine wanting to know what everybody's thinking all of the time. I mean, I can see how it would come in handy in certain circumstances, but mostly, it sounds like a huge headache. Literally.

"Why can't I hear thoughts now?" I ask.

Tristan shrugs and returns his gaze to the girls. "It might be the black magic blocking it. That's happened before. But since you called to us by accident, I'd say it's more likely you don't remember how to use it."

"Do you know how she does it? Er, I mean, how *I* do it?"

Tristan looks up at me again, his eyes dark, probably from my slip-up, then lifts his chin toward the rocking chair. "Sit down and relax. Try to blank out your own thoughts, then open your mind and feel out for mine."

I peer at him while hesitating with my butt hovering over the chair. "That's it?"

He makes it sound entirely too simple.

He shrugs again. "That's what worked the first time you learned to do it. I know it came more naturally after a while, but since I don't have the power, I can't really explain it. You said the thoughts are simply there for you to pick up on if and when you want or need to."

I drop into the chair and after a moment of staring at him, I lean back and close my eyes. After making my mind go blank, I mentally reach out toward his. I gasp at what feels like a little flicker of energy in my mind. Actually, three, although two are so light, I barely register them. I focus on the thicker one, connecting with it . . . linking with it. And Tristan's voice, sounding very much like his real one, comes in my head, singing a vaguely familiar, though old, rock song about hurricanes.

I hear you, I say with my mind.

"*I hear you, too.*"

My lids pop open, and I stare at him. His eyes flicker—a sadness crosses them again, but mostly relief and hope show in them. I try to grab the thought that went with the look, but it was too fleeting.

"What was wrong just now?"

He sighs. "Nothing. Something you apparently don't remember. But that's okay. You're making headway. See if you can pick up anyone else's mind signature."

I lift a brow.

"That's what you call people's brain waves," he explains. "You say everyone's is different, like their mental thumbprint. It allows you to identify people without actually entering their minds."

He must mean the energy flickers. "I picked up on the babies', I think."

"Not surprising. You said they're easy to read. Almost everything's physical to them."

I close my eyes and focus on one, although I can't determine which baby it belongs to.

"She adores you. I can feel that." My throat tightens. "And me. They both do."

"Of course they do. You're the best mom they could have."

I snort. How can he say that? I don't think Mom of the Year awards go to mothers who can't even remember their own children. Or let them go with the enemy.

"Do you sense any others?" he asks. "Any other mind signatures?"

I open my mind up again, but besides the three here with me, all I feel are very faint points of pressure, like little pokes not even noticeable until he said something. I shake my head. "I sense other people around us, but that's all."

Tristan's lips press together for a moment, then he stands. "I'm going to see if Teah or Teal can watch the babies. Then you and I should go for a walk."

"Um . . . okay." I don't mind the idea of getting out of this room and checking out the shelter.

He disappears and returns a few minutes later with the same dark-haired, blue-eyed girl who'd brought the babies to the medical unit earlier. "This is Teah. She and her cousin Teal babysit for us. They're also teachers."

"There's a school?" I haven't considered there being other children here.

"Yeah, but it's pretty empty now," Teah says, and her lips flatten. "The kids are all getting hit the worst. We've all been borderline dehydrated for weeks, but they're worse off. And now . . . they just can't fight it."

Tristan lifts his hand toward me, as though reaching for mine, but he quickly changes his motion and gestures toward the door. As if there's electrical energy jumping between us, I feel his hand near the small of my back as I walk out.

"It sounds like there's a crisis here," I say once we're down the stairs. "Should you be somewhere else?"

He turns to our right and begins walking. I hurry to catch up with him.

"I will soon. But you should be helping, too. Getting your memory back is a top priority. Your people need you."

Hmph. "Are you sure about that? As bad as things seem to be, they might be better off without me . . . her."

He stops in his tracks and glares at me, the hardness in his expression pulling me to a halt, too. "Don't think that for one minute, Alexis. There's a reason you were placed in the position you are. Everyone here believes in you because the Angels believe in you."

I don't argue with him. I really have no idea what he's talking about, so I don't have much of an argument. When he realizes I have no reply, he resumes walking.

"Try to reach out again and find people's mind signatures." His normally buttery voice comes out gruffly. "This is how you first learned."

As he shows me around the shelter, which he calls The Loft, I try to do just that. Again, I feel tiny, vague pokes, but nothing else. There are more in the residential area when we pass through it, but not many when we enter the vast space marked *Training*. It seems to take up at least half of the developed area of what Tristan says had once been a limestone mine and converted into a bunker by a doomsday prepper. The training section includes an archery range, a shooting range, a weight and machine room, a sparring ring, and open spaces for practicing martial arts and various weapon use. At the front, classrooms line each side, and a library section takes up the middle with bookshelves spanning the front wall.

"The people who are well are saving their energy," Tristan says as we leave the nearly empty area.

Except for a couple of die-hards on the gym equipment, the only people in here are a handful in the library. I find a big cluster of pulses in the dining area, though, and then another in the nearby medical unit. He shows me the farming space, with its acres of crops and a small barn for livestock, way in the back, surrounded by several sections of the old mine that are still undeveloped, only wide, empty spaces separated by thick pillars. It's dark here, with only a few light bulbs scattered about, and the pillars and walls are still marked from the equipment that originally dug out the limestone.

"It sounds like you're only able to sense other people like I can." He sounds disappointed, which makes me feel bad.

"Sorry." I don't know what else to say.

"It'll come."

We return to the brighter, more colorful, main part of The Loft, where someone's been working at making the place feel less like an underground bunker. There are murals painted on a few of the walls, giving the illusion that you're looking out a window. One depicts a snow-topped mountain range and another rolling green hills that meet the beach. A third, a cityscape, remains unfinished. They're all beautifully done, showing that some seriously talented residents live here. Framed pictures that have been scavenged hang on some of the interior walls, as well.

"It had been bare down here for a long time as we tried to reserve resources," Tristan says, "but the longer we stay down here, the more we realize our sanity requires something more than drab walls to look at. And the artwork gives some of us something constructive to do with our time." We come to a stop at the main intersection where the dining, training, and residential areas meet, kind of like the central square of a small town. "So, I guess that's it. The Loft."

With the tour over, we go to the kitchen to grab a late dinner. The crowd has dissipated with only a few stragglers still eating in the dining area. I wonder if he'd purposely kept me away from everyone. It probably isn't a good idea for the whole place to know their so-called leader can't remember a thing about them.

My breasts fill up again—I'm really starting to feel like a cow and hating my udders—and as if on cue, we can hear the babies' cries from the kitchen. I don't think it's normal to be able to hear them from so far away, but as Sheree said, I have super-senses. Tristan must have them, too. We make a box for our food, adding in a couple of bottles, and return to our quarters. Although there's no sun down here, I feel night has fallen. The residents are settling down, a quiet growing throughout the shelter. And we haven't yet talked about our sleeping arrangements.

"I'm not really tired," I say after finishing my meal. I'd already pumped, Tristan had fed the babies, and we'd put them down in their bed, sound asleep. "I think I'm going to go back to the library you showed me. Maybe something there will help me."

He rises to his feet, and since the room doesn't exactly have much open space, he stands right in front of me. The closeness causes electricity to zing through my nerves, and my heart picks up a quick rhythm. His tangy-sweet scent envelops me, making my head light.

"I can find another place to sleep," he says, his voice low, but I can still hear the underlying layer of hurt in it.

Unable to look up at him this close, I stare at the floor and shake my head. "No. I'm serious. I couldn't sleep right now even if I tried. I slept half the afternoon, remember? And you should sleep in your own bed."

After a moment of tension sparks between us, he moves to the side. I look back at the twins, an involuntary movement to check that they still sleep soundly, then head for the door. The sigh I hear from Tristan as I leave makes my heart squeeze. I know I'm hurting him, but I have no idea how to change that, except to do what I can to regain my memories. I try to reach my mind out for signatures as I walk, but still have no luck. He was right—sensing the others nearby is just that, *sensing* them and their physical presence. It's not the same as the flickers of mental energy I'd felt in our room, especially not like his.

After a quick stop in the kitchen to clean our dishes and bottles, I head to the library, where I find shelves and shelves of books about survival in the wild, homesteading and farming, basic technology, and military training. Almost all are non-fiction covering everything from horticulture and canning to establishing a government. I do find a couple of shelves of fiction books, however. Although I should probably be reading about leadership or something equally as helpful and relevant, I'm drawn to the novels.

The one I find most intriguing sits out on a table. A lot of people must think it's interesting, because the paperback is well-worn, with a cracked spine and dog-eared pages. I discover others in the series, and a couple of duplicates. They are the only books in the library that have multiple copies, and every single one is much loved. As I flip through the pages, I notice several passages are highlighted, most of them fight scenes, all involving supernatural characters. Notes about silver and weak spots are written in the margins.

I read the first few pages, and the story immediately sucks me in. There's something familiar about it, though, almost like a feeling of déjà vu. I must have read the book before, and some part of my subconscious mind knows it already. When the time comes, I take the book with me, stop in the kitchen for the pump, and then pause, not knowing where to go. I don't want to disturb Tristan and the babies, although if I'm aching, they'd be waking up any time now, crying with hunger. I can't bring myself to hurt him again, but know I'd be unable to stay in the room afterward.

I hate this more than he knows, more than I let on. Wandering the dark, quiet Loft by myself with these strange breasts that don't feel like my own, not knowing where to go or what to do, I feel like an alien trying to settle on a planet I know only by distant observation. I know the basics, but not who I really am or where I fit in. Except unlike the alien who's totally new, there are already set expectations for me—shoes I don't know how to fill, even if they are my own.

Not everyone's asleep. This is a place where half the residents are supernaturals who either don't need sleep or have inherent preferences for the night. Not wanting to be bothered by wandering souls, I end up in the communal bathroom, sitting on the floor with my back against the wall and trying to read while pumping. Unable to focus, I close the book and drop it facedown on the floor. A woman who looks like an older version of myself stares up at me from the back cover. I peer closer. A.K. Emerson is her name, and she has the same eyes, nose shape, and chin as me, although she has the hint of a second chin and her cheeks are much fuller than mine. She's pretty, but more like what I would look like if I were entirely human, I suppose—closer to the physical age Sheree claims me to be.

I gasp with a thought. Is this me before the *Ang'dora*, when I'd aged backwards? Is this what Tristan had been telling me before, about being a bestselling author? Somewhere deep inside, I know the truth in this, and that's why I feel like I already know the story. I'd not only read it before— I'd written it.

My chest tightens as more thoughts flood over me. I have this whole life as a bestselling author, a mom, and a wife, with friends and who knows what else? Do he and I have a good relationship? Carlie said he loves me like crazy, but do I feel the same? How long have we been together, anyway? Would he ever love me like that again? *Could* he, if I never become the Alexis he's always known? I finger the author's picture, wishing she could give me answers, as a tear rolls down my cheek.

For the first time since waking up at the edge of the lake, my situation really hits me, and I feel utterly lost and alone.

CHAPTER 7

I spend a good portion of the night wandering around The Loft while trying to push through the block that hides all of my memories before that one moment in time. But it's like a solid wall, and everything beyond it remains unreachable—any information about who I am unattainable. Several times, I come fully to the present to find myself stopped at the bottom of the stairs to our room, staring up at the door. Although I'm drawn to that place like a magnet, I can't bring myself to climb the steps. Because I know I'm drawn to *him*, but all I do is hurt him. The best I can do is sit on the wooden step, close but not too close, and read.

"You know, I have a double compartment all to myself."

The female voice startles me awake. *When did I doze off?* I straighten from leaning against the wall and look up to find Sheree's lithe body standing over me. I blink at her.

"You put all of us on your team directly around you," she says, using her long fingers to indicate the compartments on this row, including Tristan's . . . mine.

My brows furrow. "We need protection down here?"

"No. For easy access. And since I'm the only unattached person on your team, I get a place to myself. I have an extra bed is what I'm saying."

"Oh. Well, I wasn't really tired. Couldn't sleep."

"Yeah, I could tell." With a soft snort, she turns toward the end of the row. "Want some coffee or breakfast?"

The sounds of people waking and beginning their day fill The Loft as Sheree and I sit down to a breakfast of banana bread, peanut butter, and coffee. I've barely finished when I sense the twins are up. I wait as long as I can possibly stand before excusing myself to do my thing, only to round the corner and find Tristan coming down the stairs with a baby in each arm. I'd hoped they'd already left the room. We meet at the bottom of the stairs, and I force myself to lift my eyes and meet his gaze, knowing I can't avoid him forever. He seems to be scanning me for information.

"You should have come in last night," he says, and my head tilts ever so slightly on its own. "Yeah, I knew you were out here, but wanted to leave the choice to you. I'd never do anything to make you uncomfortable, Lex. I have no problem sleeping on the floor. Whatever makes you feel better. But I don't like you sleeping out here on the stairs when you have a home and a bed."

I swallow the thick lump in my throat, unable to speak. I don't know what to say. After a moment of silence, he gives a slight nod and walks in the direction from where I'd come.

"I'll take care of the twins and get some breakfast, then we have work to do," he says over his shoulder.

Part of me wants to hide in the room all day, but I know that wouldn't last long when he comes looking for me. Besides, a bigger part of me is tired of feeling so alone. Camping out in here all day wouldn't bring me answers or fix anything. So once I've dressed in a tank top and black jeans and given my hair a good brushing, I reach my mind out, trying again to find all the mind signatures surrounding me. The only one I feel, after a lot of effort and focus, is Tristan's. I begin to think we have a deeper connection than through my telepathy. Even the stone in my chest seems to warm when I reach out to him.

"As you mentioned last night, we're in crisis mode here," Tristan says a few minutes later as he leads me down the main corridor in the direction from which we'd entered only yesterday. "I don't think leaving you out of the loop will help. If we can't get your memory back, I can at least teach you and bring you up to speed. It might be the best we get."

"What do you mean?"

He pauses at the door to what he had said yesterday was my office. "As your second, I'm here to do what you can't, but part of my job is to ensure you *can* do yours. We need a contingency plan in case Owen and Blossom

48

can't figure out the antidote or remedy to your situation. And that plan is to teach you everything you need to know so you can get back to work."

"As the leader of The Loft," I say as he opens the door. If The Loft is a small town, I guess that would make me it's mayor?

He waits for me to enter first and gives a nod. "We'll start with that."

We pass through a fairly large room with folding tables arranged in a U-shape and white boards hanging on the wall that the mismatched chairs face. A list of lakes and streams mark one side of the white board, and a map has been drawn on the other side with The Loft noted in the center and bodies of water indicated around it. It's not a crude sketch or sloppy doodle, either, but created by someone with artistic talent. On the far side of the room, to the left of the white boards, Tristan opens another door. Through it we enter a much smaller room with an old, metal desk that barely leaves enough space for a chair on either side of it.

"Not quite the office you had at the mansion or the safe house, but it works." Tristan lifts his hand out to indicate the chair on the far side. "You may as well take the seat you're supposed to fill and get used to it."

My arm brushes against his as I make my way around the desk, and electricity shoots through my nerves. I pretend not to notice it and take the seat behind the desk. A slow breath leaks out of my lungs as I stare at the overwhelming mess of papers in front of me. It takes me a moment to notice there's no phone, no computer, nothing of the sort in the office.

"The digital age came to an end with the bombs and EMPs." He begins sorting through the papers. "We're back to paper and ink. You should read these and get caught up on everything."

"What are they?"

"Reports brought in while you were gone yesterday."

I look up at him, confused. "From where?"

"Everywhere we have contact throughout the world."

My chest feels tight, though I don't know why. I resort to joking. "And let me guess—brought in by courier pigeon? Or wait—by owl?"

One corner of his mouth lifts. "Falcon, actually."

My brows raise.

"Robin, a were-falcon, is one of our messengers. She's on your greater council."

I stare for a moment too long, then blink and nod. "Yeah. Of course."

Is he for freakin' real? This life—*my* life—surpasses all standards for weirdness. Sheree had mentioned my team and now Tristan refers to my greater council. They'd called me matriarch. Of what, I'm beginning to wonder. I thought they meant leader of The Loft, but now I think it's more than that.

"Tristan, what, exactly, am I leader of?"

His lips squish together in what's probably supposed to be a purse or maybe even a scowl, but makes me think of a kiss. And then I can't stop thinking about *the* kiss and how amazing it had been . . . what I would do for another. What *would* I do? That's a ridiculous thought I quickly try to shut out. Tristan's still talking but I'm too distracted to hear, except I do hear the words, "the world."

"Come again?" I say, bringing myself fully back to present.

He leans against the desk, his perfect ass settling on the edge, and I wonder what it feels like. Shit. I'm distracted again.

"Did you hear me?"

I swallow and look up at him, trying to hide the heat flushing through my body. "Sorry. A bit, uh, overwhelmed here."

He studies me for a moment, and I have to look away because everything about him distracts me. Even his voice is beautiful, deep and smooth like warm honey and butter, but at least I can allow myself to focus on that.

"You're the Amadis matriarch and leader of Earth's Angels. The Angels have placed you in charge of protecting and helping everything here on Earth. So basically, the world is yours."

My gaze shoots up at him. "Say that again?"

He sighs. "I know it's all new to you, but can you please focus? We have a lot of work to do."

"Oh, no, I heard you this time. At least, I think I did. I'm just trying to make sure the words you said were the same ones I heard. Because I thought when you all called me matriarch and leader, you meant of this place. Like somehow I'd been elected mayor or whatever of The Loft. But that's not what you said. Is it?"

He shakes his head. "No."

I listen intently as he gives me a quick history lesson—my history. My bloodline had led the Amadis, the Angels' army on Earth, since its beginning, so I'd been in line to take over as matriarch when I was born. By the time the war had started, I'd taken on that role. When we won the war, the Angels themselves told us I was to lead the effort in helping humanity to rebuild.

"That's the gist of it," Tristan finishes, although I feel like he held a lot back. He'd said everything matter-of-factly, as though reciting a section in a history book, withholding the personal parts, the emotions, of everything that had happened.

I stare at the papers on the desk, snatches of words floating through my mind as I try to comprehend.

"That's . . . um . . ." I take a deep breath and let it out slowly. "Overwhelming is a bit of an understatement." Questions flood over me, too many and too fast to pick one. So I take his lead and try to focus on the task at hand—my current role. I look up at him again. "What does it exactly mean? What do I actually *do*?"

The explanation never included the words "rule the world," but the implication hangs from each sentence. How does one person rule the entire world, anyway? Especially in what has practically become the Dark Ages? How is it even possible?

"You've been following the Angels' lead with a philosophy of interfering only when necessary. And so far, with the majority of the population remaining under the Earth's surface, where it's safer, we haven't had to do much but monitor and assist when needed, such as with Demons." He taps a finger on the pile of papers. "These reports will give you updated information from our sources. Some places have had a few issues, but you've given them direction. Honestly, things have run pretty smoothly."

"Direction or orders?" I mutter, still trying to grasp my role as leader . . . of the entire damn world.

"Direction," Tristan replies, though it had been a rhetorical question not even meant for him to hear. "That's the kind of leader you've been, and it's worked so far. That will likely change when more people return to the surface, and when it does, I know you'll be up for it."

I snort. "You sound a lot more confident than I feel."

He chuckles. "It's always been that way, but I've never doubted you, Lex. I've always seen the greatness in you. You've only recently discovered it for yourself, especially during that final battle. You really came into your own then—became what the rest of us had been waiting for. And I know you will again."

He places his hand over mine for a brief moment—long enough for sparks to shoot up my arm—before he seems to remember himself. He withdraws it and leaves me with the pile of reports to peruse.

I can hardly believe what I read. First of all, I'd been spelling Amadis in my head phonetically, like Uhmahdeese, but that's wrong. And what I'd heard as Daymahnee is spelled Daemoni. The reports come from members of the Amadis, which is comprised of the supernaturals who consider themselves on the good side, soldiers of the Angels' army. Tristan has already clarified that the Daemoni are the opposite—the Demons' army. The reports also mention the Demons and Earth's Angels, as well as what they refer to as newly discovered and developed species, including dragons and a variety of fae.

Mostly, however, the reports relay information about underground communities, some Norman and some a mix of Norman and Amadis. They've figured out new ways to grow food, repurpose items to produce electricity or filter water or provide some other need that had been destroyed by the collapse of infrastructure. There are some needs listed— items that are no longer being produced in factories but have to be scavenged. From what I can gather, the were-falcon and other messengers bring these needs lists to us, and we somehow provide from here. I'll have to find out how that's done.

Tristan explains when he brings me lunch. "We send the messages out to our contacts, and if anyone has an item someone else needs, they let us know. Then Owen creates portals to transport the items."

"Sounds like that could take eons."

He nods as he chews a bite of his lunch. "That's where we are right now. Hopefully, some day, we'll be able to rebuild to where we used to be, only better."

"But for now we're literally in the Dark Ages."

He gives me a small smile. "That's not what the Angels call it. They've declared this the Age of Angels."

"Guess that sounds promising."

"Hope is what we all need right now."

I can't argue with that.

When night comes, Tristan convinces me to sleep in our compartment. He sleeps on the floor, as promised, and of course, I feel as guilty as I knew I would. But apparently, I've needed the sleep, because guilt or no, I'm out like a light.

"You slept in your room last night," Blossom notes the next morning when she joins me for breakfast. "I take that as a good sign."

I frown. "I guess, but it's weird. I feel bad for Tristan for making him sleep on the floor."

She focuses on spreading peanut butter on her toast. "You know, I could put up a magical barrier in the middle of the bed so you can both sleep on it without getting close. But wouldn't that be weirder? I mean, you're married. Maybe you should try living normally, like a married couple would do. It might help with your memories."

"You know what would help with her memories?" Tristan asks as he sets two baby carriers on the table and then sits down. "If you and Owen figured out the damn antidote."

Blossom looks at him with wide eyes—bigger than her already large ones. His words aren't surprising, so it must be his harsh tone. Tristan plants his elbows on the table and drops his forehead against the heels of his palms. His shoulders rise and fall with deep breaths.

"Sorry," he mutters. He stands back up and grabs a baby carrier in each hand. "I miss my wife. They miss their mother."

Leaving his untouched plate behind, he strides off with the twins. I blink against the burn in my eyes and push my own half-eaten food away. A small but warm hand lands on mine.

"We'll fix you, don't worry," Blossom assures. Then she stands. "I'll get back to work right now. Owen's been up all night and needs relief."

I watch her walk away but only have a moment to feel sorry for myself before a blonde vampire drops into the seat in front of me.

"Good morning," Vanessa says, the joy in her voice laced with a sharp edge, as though cheerfulness isn't quite natural for her. "You look like you could use a good fight. Want to spar?"

We go to the boxing ring in the nearly empty training area, and once we start, the moves come naturally to me. She knows exactly what I need —the physical release of slamming my fist into something and the pain that answers. We've only gone a couple of rounds, though, before Vanessa's called to a real fight.

CHAPTER 8

I feel the mental jab in my head at the same time Vanessa's walkie-talkie squelches from the side of the boxing ring. *We need Vanessa* pops into my mind in Tristan's voice at the same time Owen's comes over the speaker.

"We've got an Earth's Angel and a vamp nearby and in possible trouble. Want to fight some real Demons?" Owen asks over the radio.

"Ten-four. On my way," Vanessa answers, and I run after her, up the tunnel toward the door to the outside.

Owen and Tristan already stand there, along with a naked woman with broad shoulders, a barrel chest, narrow hips and thin legs, a beak-like nose, and round, dark eyes. She looks like a red-headed bird. Tristan calls her Robin, and I burst into laughter. When she, Tristan, and Owen silently stare at me, I realize that's her real name and bite my lip to sober myself. But I sense Vanessa holding back her own snickers.

"You stay here," Tristan says to me as the first door to the outside begins to open.

"Let her come," Vanessa says.

"So something else can happen to her? She probably doesn't even remember how to fight."

Vanessa rolls her eyes. "I was just in the sparring ring with her. Trust me. She remembers. Besides, maybe a knock upside the head will do her good."

Tristan lets out a low growl, but doesn't stop me when I enter the dark in-between space with them. As soon as the outside door opens, I know without a doubt I'm going. I haven't realized how much I've needed fresh air until I inhale a huge gulp of it.

"They're on the other side of that far hill." Robin points to a hill in the distance, several miles away. "There's a white farm house at the bottom and an abandoned town not too far away."

"I know the place," Owen says.

"Good. I have to keep going." With that, she explodes into a falcon and flies away in the other direction. Feathers and some kind of goo rain to the ground where she'd stood only a moment ago.

Owen disappears with a *pop*. Tristan glares at me and shakes his head, but when Vanessa *pops* out of sight, too, I instinctively jump after her. My vision goes black, and my lungs seem to collapse as the air's sucked out of me. But only for a brief moment, the blink of an eye. Then I suddenly stand on the side of a hill with Vanessa, Owen, and Tristan. Disoriented, I immediately stumble forward. A jolt of electricity shoots through my arm as my elbow's caught by a large hand.

"Guess you remember how to flash," Tristan mutters as he jerks me back to my feet.

Right below us but hovering in the air, a man with brown, feathery wings fights with a half-dozen beasts with wings of their own. Only, theirs are featherless and membranous, made of the same leathery skin that stretches over their muscular bodies, and the wing's points end in talons. Horns protrude from their heads, and they sport hooves instead of feet. Owen wasn't kidding when he said real Demons.

"Catch," Vanessa says at the same time she flicks something silver my way.

My hand shoots out and catches a dagger by the hilt. Tristan and I both look at her.

"I grabbed it from your room, just in case you wanted a real fight," she says with a shrug. "Looks like you did."

"Shield her, Owen," Tristan orders, and Owen's hands rub together before flicking out toward me. A whoosh of air surrounds me, making my ears pop.

"Go for their throats," Vanessa says. "You have to decapitate them."

"Except she can't fly." Tristan's big black and silver wings burst from his back. At that thought, mine appear, too, but he's right. I hide them with another thought so they won't get in my way.

"We'll bring them down to your level then." Vanessa disappears into a blur.

The streak of her movement springs into the air toward a low-hovering Demon, and she brings him down to the ground. I sprint to them, but it frees itself before I can reach it. We both jump after it. I jab my blade deep into the thick hide of its thigh and hang on with my left hand as I swing my other arm up to latch onto its wing. I grab on to what feels like cartilage under the smooth skin, shove my feet into its side, and launch myself backward while twisting. The cartilage in my hand snaps, the skin of the wing tears, and the monster lets out a deep, guttural cry. We barely hit the ground when I lunge for my dagger still lodged in its leg. I jerk the blade free, spin, and slice it across the Demon's throat. It lets out a disgustingly sour breath of sulfur before the head tumbles off its body. Its arms catch the horned sphere, and the thing disappears.

"Not your best, but it worked," Vanessa says before turning to the next one.

We dispatch all of the Demons in a few minutes, leaving only the brown-winged man.

"Thanks for the help." He eyes each of us until his light blue eyes fall on me. "I was coming to see you, Alexis. Noah sent me."

I barely hear his words as a wave of something unsettling washes over me, lifting the hair on the back of my neck. *Evil.* There's another one, hiding behind a bush. I lunge that way, and my fist latches on to a figure crouching behind there. Another wave of evil shoots through me. I pull my arm back, about to stab it with my dagger.

"Wait! She's with me," the man yells.

I freeze—of my own doing, not Tristan's—as I take in the figure. She's not a Demon, but a small woman with long, dark blonde curls, staring up at me with big, blue eyes full of fear. Fangs protrude from under her lips, and her eyes turn from dark blue to bright red. I spring off of her, landing on my feet several yards away.

"But she's evil," I whisper.

"She wants to be converted," the guy says.

I spin on him. I don't know what that means. My mouth opens, but Tristan gives a slight shake of his head.

"Is this why the Demons were after you?" Tristan asks the man as he waves his hand in the air. The woman's body goes stiff. I know that look on her face. Tristan has paralyzed her with his power. He doesn't trust her, either.

"Probably," the guy answers. "Or maybe for the delivery Noah has for you."

He flicks his hand, and a large messenger bag flies out from behind the bush where the girl had been hiding. It lands in his hand, and he swings the strap over his head.

"Lead the way," he says.

"Who are you?" Tristan demands.

"Oh, yeah, sorry, man. Call me Cam." He holds out his hand to Tristan and gives him a smile, dimples popping in his cheeks. "This is Emma. She was turned by the Daemoni during the war, but she's not one of them. She wants to be converted. She deserves to be."

Tristan studies the vampire with narrowed eyes. Then he finally gives a small nod.

"We'll take her in."

We flash back to The Loft's entrance, then Owen and Vanessa lead us all inside. Tristan uses his power to direct the vampire's floating body through the tunnel, but Cam stays close by her side. He must be what I'd read and heard so much about—an Earth's Angel, like Tristan and me.

"Sheree will be happy for something to do," Vanessa says to Owen, who agrees.

We go down the first hall from the storage area to where *Conversion Center* is printed on the door. The area inside is large, but divided into rooms by curtains and cardboard tacked to two-by-fours. A desk made of filing cabinets with a wooden door across them sits by the entry. We stop there, just inside the center. I sense nobody here.

"Alexis, can you—" Tristan cuts himself off when he looks at me and lets out a short sigh. "Vanessa, find Sheree. Owen . . ."

He holds his hands up, stopping Tristan. "I know, I know. Time to get back to work."

"Wait," Cam says as he reaches into the large bag hanging at his side. "Noah said you're the one to give this to. He said if anyone could figure out the magic surrounding it, you could."

He pulls out a statue over two feet tall and sets it on the makeshift desk, which groans under the weight. An ancient-looking, stony gargoyle with a dragon-like head stares blankly at us, its mouth perpetually open to bare its fangs and wings forever lifting from its back. The gray stone is stained black in many places, wearing a thin beard of moss in others, and weathered everywhere.

"Came from a cathedral in England," Cam says. "Or maybe it was Scotland?" His brows squeeze together for a moment, and then he shrugs. "Noah gave it to me to bring to you, because it's obviously no ordinary gargoyle."

Owen studies it for a moment, then moves his hands over it. "There's heavy magic, for sure. Some darkness to it, too. I can—"

"Owen," Tristan interrupts. "Priorities."

Owen straightens and nods. "It'll have to wait."

He hurries out of the room, leaving a perplexed Cam.

"Who's Noah?" I ask, and Cam's brows dive deeper down his forehead.

Tristan's nostrils flare as he inhales a deep breath.

"Your uncle." Cam's tone makes my question sound dumb. Oops. I probably know Noah. My uncle. No wonder Tristan's upset. He doesn't want Cam, or anyone, knowing about my memory loss. The newcomer looks from me to Tristan and back to me. "What's going on?"

Sheree walks in at that moment, and the orders she starts barking send Cam's question into the dark corners of oblivion, hopefully lost forever. Tristan sets the vampire, Emma, up on a bed behind one of the curtains, and he and Sheree begin shackling her with silver cuffs.

"That's not necessary," Cam says.

"It's for her own good." Sheree clamps one of the latches into place. "This won't be easy on her, and we don't want her to hurt herself or do something she'll regret later. You all should go. Unless you want to stay and help, Alexis?"

Tristan clinches a hand over Cam's shoulder and steers him away, although the guy doesn't look like he wants to take two steps from the girl's side.

"She won't want you to see her like this," Tristan says as he forcibly moves Cam through the door and out of the Conversion Center. "Trust me. I know."

When they're gone, Sheree double-checks the shackles around Emma's wrists and ankles, then squeezes the vampire's forearm. The girl's body trembles and bucks.

"You're the best at giving Amadis power," Sheree says to me. "You have the most. Want to give it a try?"

She directs me how to push my good Amadis power into the girl as we try to shove out her evil Daemoni energy. I'm no good at it right now, though, but I stay with Sheree for a while, watching the conversion begin to take effect. Tristan's right—if this Cam and Emma are a thing, she wouldn't want him to see her like this. Horrible fails to describe the experience properly as the worst of her evil shows itself in the forms of bloodcurdling screams and threats of gory deaths—ours—before she finally settles into a comatose state.

"She'll receive faith healing next," Sheree explains. "But we'll have more rounds of this to go. I can do this myself. She's not all that bad and should be an easy conversion."

After what I'd seen, I'd hate to see a difficult one.

I sit with Sheree for the rest of the day and evening except when I have to take care of boob issues. She tells me about other conversions we've done together, trying to jog my memory. I enjoy hanging out with her—I feel like she doesn't really expect anything from me, especially any more than I can offer in my current state of mind. It's a nice reprieve from the constant pressure I feel from the others. Especially Tristan.

When I return to our apartment, I take Blossom's advice and convince Tristan to sleep in the bed. It's awkward as hell, each of us hovering on the edge of our sides so as to not encroach on the other. Once he falls asleep, he tosses and turns for hours, keeping me awake until the babies relieve him of the torture at some insanely early hour of the morning. After feeding them and putting them back to bed, he disappears.

CHAPTER 9

"*B*eing leader of the world or whatever you call it seems to be boring as hell," I say to Tristan. I've spent nearly the whole afternoon perusing the reports I hadn't gone through the other day, and he's come to check on me. "Are you sure this is all we can do? Shouldn't we be doing more?"

He leans against the doorjamb and pushes his hands into his jeans front pockets. The corded muscles of his forearms tighten, their power obvious. The man has one hell of a body and brains to go with the brawn. His cranky personality could use improvement . . . although that probably has more to do with me than with him.

"After everything they experienced, with all of the hate and all of the blood spilled, humanity has been as peaceful as they could possibly be," he says. "There's been a few skirmishes and issues here and there, but really, everyone wants to settle back into a new normal. That's what they've been working on. Besides, they're all underground, too afraid to venture out yet. Believe me, once that starts happening, I'm sure our jobs will become much more interesting."

"So these directions, as you called them, that I've been giving . . ." I twirl my hand in the air over the pile of papers. "Do you really think that's the best I can do?"

"You don't remember, but one of my talents is to easily be able to identify the best solution if I'm aware of enough facts. Based on what we know, yes, you're doing the best you can do. The best anyone can do."

"But shouldn't I be building cities and governments or something? Doing more for the people to get this world back to the way it was?"

He lifts an eyebrow. "Is that what's best for humanity? The way it was?"

I sigh. "As if I would remember. I just know it had to have been better than this life."

His head tilts to the side. "Lots of people would disagree. What happened to the world was horrific, and this life is harder, but our world was pretty messed up before. Many people say the reset button has been hit, and we've been given a chance to start over and be better." He pauses and straightens. "Anyway, you're not meant to establish a new world order and rule with an iron fist, Alexis. That's not you, and that's not the Angels. Not something they would want or expect. You're doing exactly what the world needs right now. And like I said, soon enough, it will need more, and you will be there for it. We all will be."

I gnaw on my bottom lip as my gaze slides over the papers. He sounds so confident, not only in me, but in everyone's support of me. At least, of the real Alexis. I can't help but wonder if he really feels that way about her or if he's simply trying to make me feel better about things so I'll worry more about the problems directly in front of us.

"If you're done here, I thought we could help out in the kitchen tonight," Tristan says, his tone much lighter than it had been.

I look up at him, surprised. "Uh, yeah, sure. Why not? They need help serving?"

"Nah. We'll be cooking."

My brows shoot up with more shock. "You want *me* to *cook*? Wait . . . do I know how to cook? Do *you*?"

He smiles, and whether it's forced or not, I don't care. It knocks me off my feet. Seriously. I'd started to stand when he flashed that grin, but I fall back into my seat, a gasp caught in my throat. He jerks his head toward the outer door, his light brown hair swinging across his square jaw.

"Come on. It'll be fun. I promise."

As soon as we walk into the kitchen and Tristan makes it clear that we'll be cooking with the others in here, a murmur of excitement passes through all the workers. Someone puts some music on, and then everyone moves out of our way, keeping busy with their own tasks while helping out when we need them. They chop and stir and sway on their feet to the music's beat. Tristan has to tell me what to do each step of the way, which starts to earn sideways glances from the others. At first, they laugh,

61

thinking he's teasing with all of his bossiness, but then I can feel their confusion growing. From their whispered exchanges, I realize we cook with them on a regular basis and we're normally a team, moving in synchronicity with each other. From what I gather, not only can I cook, but so can Tristan, and we're very good at it. My current ignorance causes suspicion.

"We had a bet," Tristan tells everyone as we finish up the newly invented dish that would feed everyone using as little water as possible. "Alexis claimed I couldn't teach an idiot how to cook a decent meal, and she volunteered to be the idiot."

I narrow my eyes at him. He throws me a look, a teasing smile on his lips and a plea for cooperation in his eyes.

"So," he says to the others when I don't protest, "did I win?"

Most of the staff, all females, nod and praise him, telling him what a spectacular job he did and begging him to teach them his ways. Tristan lays his arm over my shoulders and pulls me into his side, making my brain forget to order my lungs to breathe. In fact, my brain forgets nearly everything the entire time he holds me.

"To be fair," he says to everyone, "Alexis isn't an idiot, even when she tries. But I'll take the win."

He laughs as all the women giggle and cheer. I look up at him and shake my head as he receives the ego boost. He probably needs it with everything going on—or not going on—between us. He winks at me, and my mind is suddenly gone. Wiped out. Erased. His mouth stretches into a grin in response to the blank look I give him, and I realize he's been holding back on all the smiles he's given me before. They're nothing compared to this genuine one.

My heart suddenly aches with the need to remember our past, our history, our present. My soul throbs with the emptiness, the dark place that I know used to be filled with us, with our love.

He sees something in my eyes, though. In my face. Because the beautiful grin dissolves. The spark leaves his eyes. His arm drops from around me, and he steps away, putting distance between us. I instantly feel cold and lonely.

"Let's eat," he calls out, and the group bursts into organized chaos, preparing to serve the several hundred residents of The Loft.

When we're finally able to eat, Tristan and I join a table of those we call family and friends. Owen, Vanessa, Blossom, Jax, Sheree, Carlie, and a few others whose names I should know sit at the large, round table. Although everyone seems to be in a jovial mood, telling all kinds of funny war stories, I sense the tension lying under the surface. They're all worried, but trying to cover it up as they work to tell then explain inside jokes and crazy situations we'd been in and gotten out of together. And then I realize what they're doing—trying to bring my memories back.

As they laugh about yet another story, I feel as though I'm drifting away from them. I still sit in the same seat between Blossom and Tristan, but at the same time, I feel completely removed from them. Their voices fade into the distance, blending together and becoming background noise. My gaze travels from each face, not only at our table, but at all the tables in the dining room, all of them full. And I don't really feel like I belong. I'm a stranger among friends. A newcomer to this tight-knit community. Someone they don't really want here. They want her, not me. I'm an intruder. An imposter. They want the real thing. But what if she's gone forever?

Surrounded by a sea of people, I feel like an island.

"*Alexis, where'd you go?*" Tristan's voice fades back in, but I can't tell if it comes through my ears or . . . my mind.

Then, as though I'm dropped into a stadium at the moment of a big score, the voices lift in a rush of noise around me. Except not around me . . . *in* me. In my head. Dozens of voices at once, hundreds of them, rising into a cacophony of words and an assault of images flooding into my mind.

I throw my arms over my head and squeeze my eyes shut, trying to block it all out. I fling myself forward, doubling over, and bang my forehead on the edge of the table. Lights prick behind my eyelids, wiping all the images away.

And everything falls silent.

When I open my eyes, I'm surprised to find myself still surrounded by people. Tristan's right in front of me, his mouth moving but no sound reaching my ears. I blink and try to focus.

"*Lex, are you okay? Are you with us?*" His words come first in my mind and then audibly. Everyone else's voices follow, but I tune them out. With my ears, anyway.

"*Is she back?*" The question's in Sheree's voice, but not really. It sounds kind of like her, but with a different quality. Almost like she speaks through a paper towel tube.

"*Maybe she's okay now, and we don't have to worry about the antidote we can't seem to figure out.*" Blossom's voice, and she carries on with a nonstop internal monologue.

Vanessa's mind is filled with a surprising amount of worry mixed with a little hope that Alexis might be back to normal. And Owen's all over the hope. I grab glimpses of him and Blossom in a softly lit workroom, slaving over a table covered in bottles, jars, and vials. He'd begun to wonder if they'd ever figure out what's wrong with me.

"Alexis? Are you with us?" Tristan speaks aloud, his voice catching my attention. I look back at him. Concern fills his voice and his face.

"Um . . . yeah." I clear my throat, then try what we haven't done in a couple of days. *I think my telepathy's back. Like, all the way.*

His brows lift immediately. He hears me. "*I should have known. Are you okay?*"

It's really fucking weird.

He chuckles and draws his attention to the others. He speaks quietly, only for those closest around us to hear. "She's still not back, but her telepathy is."

"With a vengeance," I mutter as I massage my temples.

"That's a good sign," Sheree says. "Right?"

"It's a start," Tristan agrees.

Owen and Blossom trade apprehensive grins. Vanessa simply observes me with narrow, icy eyes and arms crossed over her chest.

"Try me," she demands. Everyone looks at her with wide eyes and parted mouths, and she shrugs. "Let's see if it's really back. Read my mind."

Uneasy, I look around at the others. Tristan gives me a small nod of encouragement. So I focus my mind on sensing everyone else. Little flicks of energy pop up all around. They must be what Tristan had called mind signatures. Each one is unique, although some have similarities with others. I'll have to figure out the connection later because Vanessa glares at me with expectation. *What's her problem?* I immediately identify her mind signature, pick up on the energy, and follow it to her thought. I find nothing but white space at first, then images of changing shapes and colors, like a kaleidoscope.

Are you purposely blocking me? I ask her.

A slow smile stretches her ruby lips. "*Do you really think I'd let you see what's going on in this beautiful mind of mine?*"

Then why'd you insist on being my test subject?

"*This is not my favorite part about you. I had to know for sure so I could put my defenses back up. It's been an admittedly nice break the last few days.*"

Why? Did she jump into your mind a lot?

Her grin dissipates. "*Not at all. But I'm not one to take chances like that.*"

In other words, she doesn't trust Alexis . . . me.

"*Don't take it personally. I don't trust anyone.*"

I frown. She'd heard my thoughts. I'd neglected to turn mine off from her. I need to figure out how to control this ability before everyone knows everything that passes through my mind. Thankfully, everyone wants to practice with me. Owen and Blossom disappear right after they finish eating, but Tristan, Sheree, Jax, and Carlie all have full conversations with me without any of us opening our mouths. By the time we return to our room for the evening, my head pounds, and I'm mentally exhausted.

The babies distract me from my troubles. After pumping, I help Tristan feed and bathe them, then we sit on the floor and play with them. Their big brown eyes light up as they stare at us, kicking their feet and waving their fists in the air. They coo and smile at us, and when they think we aren't paying attention to them, they babble at each other. With the sounds they make and the way they pause, they seem to be having their own private conversation. I check their minds, and their thoughts come in the same gibberish. Tristan and I listen to them and whisper guesses at what they're saying as they carry on for a while. Then they suddenly stop, and they both twist their bodies until they roll over. They grin at each other, then squirm some more. Elliana manages to pull her legs under her stomach, but as much as she tries, she can't push her chest off the floor. The struggle maddens her, and the grunts of frustration quickly melt into a screaming fit. I pick her up and nuzzle my face into her neck, turning her whimpers into giggles. Then Tristan and I play peek-a-boo with both of them, and they break into loud belly laughs.

The. Best. Sound. Ever.

With all the loneliness I've been feeling, who knew these two tiny humans could make it all go away? By the time I fall into my side of the bed, I feel a hundred times better than I have all day. Than I have since I woke up that day by the lake.

Tristan must feel better also, because he sleeps well, meaning I do, too. The sound of squeaky babies wakes me up early in the morning. As my mind drags itself out of a nice, deep sleep, it slowly takes note of my surroundings—my immediate surroundings. The arm laying over my side. The fingers pressing into my hip right along my underwear line. The large, warm body against my back, and the breath on my neck and ear. I freeze as his fingers curl up and down along that sensitive area where my thigh and pelvis meet, the tips skating oh-so-near the middle before pulling back, sending waves of heat and tingles through my nerves. He comes close again, and now a growing hardness presses into my ass. I can't help the whimper that escapes at the same time my pelvis involuntarily rocks against him.

"What the—shit!" Tristan springs away, landing on his feet on the far side of the bed. "I'm so . . . I'm sorry."

Before I can reply and without another word, he strides out the door wearing a pair of workout pants and shoes in his hands. I lie back and let out a long breath while pushing my hand through my hair and staring at the ceiling. My whole body aches and throbs for more of his touch. What a traitor it is.

CHAPTER 10

The babies start crying moments later, bringing Tristan right back through the door. We do the morning routine I'm growing accustomed to without a word, probably because of the five-foot thick wall of tension between us. The awkwardness pisses me off. We'd been so comfortable with each other last night, and now, I feel like he hates me again. Not until after breakfast and we drop the girls with Teah and Teal does he speak to me, and only to tell me we need to see how Owen and Blossom are coming along. Yep. He's pissed at me, at my memory loss.

He leads me to a section past the dining area and near the medical unit, and when we enter through a doorway into a small room, we find the same scene I'd seen in Owen's memory last night. He and Blossom are hunched over a wooden workbench. Papers, vials, tubes, and various lab equipment are scattered over the table. On one end sits a makeshift Bunsen burner—a metal bowl hovering over a flame that dances in a saucer, although what fuels the flame, I can't see. Liquid inside the bowl bubbles and gurgles. A chaotic mixture of scents fills the air, making my nose twitch.

"Anything yet?" Tristan asks the pair. They don't even look up from their work.

"Yeah, but it's . . . disturbing," Owen says.

"It's not entirely bad," Blossom counters.

Tristan and I move to their sides to see what they're working on. Their hands hover over small bowls of water, moving side to side.

"What is it?" Tristan asks when they don't continue.

After another moment, they both drop their hands and finally look at us.

"The water's clean," Blossom announces. "Not even the slightest bit of magic, dark or otherwise, taints that water, which is a miracle."

"The samples from the lake?" Tristan clarifies.

"Yep. We've tested every last drop they brought back, in every way possible. It seems to be a viable source of water for The Loft." She frowns, though, and looks at me. "But the bad news . . . this means we don't know what's wrong with you. Whatever happened to you, it's not from the water."

"Because I didn't let you drink it," Owen says emphatically, although not quite as proudly as I would have expected, considering how doubtful Tristan has been. "But that means we need to figure out what *did* happen to you."

"Something in the air?" Tristan asks.

Owen pulls a face. "That only affected Alexis? We were all there, but nothing happened to the rest of us."

"Something has happened to our other scouts, though," Blossom says. "The groups that went out before you all did and never returned. It must have been the same thing, but if they all ended up like Alexis, nobody would have known to come back here. They could be wandering around like lost little kids."

"If those beasts didn't kill them already," Owen mutters, his voice dark. "My dad . . ." He pauses and grimaces, before continuing. "I'd heard stories of the dragons being real, but I thought they were like the norms' stories—myths made up to entertain and scare little children so they'd behave and not run off."

Dragons? I'd read about them being seen in a few of my reports. Is that what we'd seen the other day?

"Could this be from the dragon?" Tristan asks. "What happened to Alexis?"

Owen shakes his head. "I don't think so. It didn't show up until after she woke up."

Tristan rakes his hand through his hair, pulling the locks away from his face. "We have no choice. You'll have to go back out there. Same team, since they managed to return this time. Maybe you're all immune to whatever it was."

"And Alexis isn't?" Doubt fills Blossom's voice. "You guys are immune to just about everything."

Tristan grimaces. "It doesn't make sense, but none of this does. Tomorrow, you go out, Owen. First thing. I'd go with you—"

Owen cuts him off. "We don't need both of you out of commission."

Tristan nods and turns toward the door without even a cursory glance toward me. I prepare to follow him anyway.

"Wait," Blossom says, her hand wrapping around my forearm to stop me. "We did want you to try this. It's an antidote for just about every poisonous potion. Kind of like the norms' penicillin but for magic."

She hands me a mug full of liquid that smells like dirt. I reluctantly drink it. They all stare at me expectantly as several minutes tick by. Eventually, I can only shake my head.

"We didn't expect it to be so easy," Blossom says with a sigh, "but we had to try."

Owen holds out a jug. "We made a batch for sick bay. I'm sure Carlie can use it."

Tristan takes the jug, and he heads for the medical unit with me right behind him. We find an overcrowded waiting area.

"I hope this works," Carlie says, her voice low as we follow her to a back room. "Some of these people seem more than dehydrated. I think we have a virus going around."

"Great," Tristan mutters under his breath. "Exactly what we need right now."

"We *need* water," Carlie says. "I can't prescribe the usual 'drink plenty of liquids' when there are no liquids to drink."

Tristan runs a hand over his face. "Maybe by tomorrow we'll have something."

"Hopefully, we can make it that long before this thing spreads like wildfire." Carlie's pink lips turn down with worry.

"Let's get everyone who's sick quarantined and try to control it."

I don't know what to do while they make plans, so I stay out of the way and practice my telepathy. I do as Tristan had suggested so many days ago and feel out for people's mind signatures. This time I can easily pick them up, and I work on getting to know them. I start to differentiate between Norman mind signatures and those belonging to supernaturals, and I determine Owen's and Blossom's, who are mages, are similar but differ quite a bit from Sheree's, a shifter, and the quality of hers is not the same as Vanessa's, a vampire. I'm quickly able to distinguish the various species—norm, vampire, shifter, and mage—and feel a twinge of pride. And hope.

Picking out mind signatures is one thing; actually listening to people's thoughts without their permission or even knowledge is another. I try to be respectful of their privacy. I really do. But some thoughts are entirely too juicy. After listening to several in a row wondering what the hell's wrong with me and coming up with their own freaky theories, though, I realize why listening to people's random thoughts isn't such a good idea—you just might learn something you're better off not knowing. Not that it stops me.

The idea that maybe I can remember more about myself from others' thoughts and memories seems too good to ignore. Although most people haven't a single iota of a thought about me, I'm pleased to discover not everyone who does thinks I'm a basket case. In general, I'd say the thoughts of the people of The Loft about Alexis are . . . conflicting. There's a lot of admiration and respect, but also a lot of concern, especially with the current state of the community. Some think I should be doing a better job taking care of them.

"Can we talk?" I ask Tristan after he and Carlie finish up their strategy discussion. He frowns, and I realize he probably thinks I mean about what happened this morning. No way am I going there. I open my mouth to explain, but a familiar voice screams in my head.

"Alexis! Tristan! Need help!" Sheree yells, and when I latch onto her mind signature, I notice a brand new one with her—one that hadn't been there moments ago when I'd checked on her and doesn't belong to anyone I've identified so far.

"It'll have to wait," Tristan says to me, before taking off in a jog through the medical unit and out the door. I follow on his heels.

We rush to the Conversion Center, where Vanessa meets us at the door. She swings it open and holds it for us. We hurry into the front room to find Sheree standing there, her face full of shock, with a naked man standing in front of her. Cam's there, too, although he doesn't look quite as surprised.

"Who are you?" Tristan demands of the strange man who stands nearly as tall as himself.

"Where'd you come from?" Vanessa asks at the same time.

The man's dark, shaggy hair hangs in his face, partially covering bright, blue eyes that stare at Sheree. The woman's eyes widen as they lock with his, and her skin flushes a dark pink.

"He . . . he, uh . . ." She stammers as she waves her misshapen, almost paw-like hands in the air without tearing her eyes from his. "He just appeared here. Out of nowhere!"

My brows furrow with confusion. Sheree should know about flashing. She's supernatural herself. Why is she freaking out about it? She's a shifter, too, so surely she has no problems with nudity. Or maybe she does . . . It's not like I know her very well.

"How'd you get in here?" Tristan barks, and now I'm super confused. He stands in a fighting stance, his muscles coiled and prepared for action, as though he might pounce on the guy at any moment. He holds his hand up, palm toward the stranger, paralyzing him. My confusion only grows. Why are they all surprised by this man's sudden appearance? Isn't this normal for these people? Why are they so uptight about it? Tristan looks ready for a fight.

I hadn't even noticed Vanessa left until she suddenly appears by my side again, my hair lifting off my shoulder from the breeze.

"I checked with Owen," she says. "Shield's up. Wards are in place. Nobody can flash in or out of here."

Oh. That's why.

As though that announcement wakes her up, Sheree's eyes finally break free from the man's and drift over to the table behind him. Then they grow even wider than before.

"Oh my god!" she shrieks.

Cam laughs at the same time. "So you're the gargoyle," he says easily.

Sheree looks back at the man then at the table again. Her hand flies to her mouth, claws protruding from her fingers. "*You?*"

The man's full lips curl into a small smile. When he speaks, we're all taken aback by the Scottish accent. "I've been watching you, lass. Thought it was time to meet. I am Aidan Craig." He glances at her lengthening claws. "No worries. You can put those away. I stand on your side."

"I don't sense Amadis," Tristan says.

"We've always stayed outside the confines of the Amadis *and* the Daemoni," Aidan says.

"We?" Tristan asks.

"My clan. My kind. The gargoyles. We serve the Angels directly, protecting mankind, since the first one of us was created." The man's blue eyes darken to a stormy gray, and his gaze falls to the floor. "I know not where the rest are. For near two centuries, I've been petrified and attached to the Glasgow Cathedral, when Lucifer captured Goji, our creator. Thanks to the dragons. The fookin' bastards. They probably took my family."

"What do you know of the dragons?" Tristan asks, a new curiosity in his voice.

Aidan eyes him. "They are evil fookers. And greedy. They will not hesitate to kill to protect their treasure. They are not to be trusted . . . fah . . ."

His words dissolve into incomprehensible grunts, and his voice trails off. Then his entire body freezes, and the color of his skin drains away, leaving him as gray as a corpse. Before any of us can react, his body turns to stone and shrinks down into the gargoyle Cam had first brought to us. We all stare at it in silence for a long, drawn-out moment.

"Well, son of a bitch," Cam says, breaking the silence.

"Hey." Tristan raps his knuckles on the gargoyle's head. "Come back."

The edges of the stony statue seem to blur for a moment, but then it falls perfectly still again.

"If he's been petrified for nearly two hundred years, maybe he's having a hard time holding his shape," Sheree says.

"Do you know anything about gargoyles?" Vanessa asks with a light brow raised.

Sheree throws her annoyed look. "No, but I do know about shifters. The longer you're in one form, the harder it is to transform and hold the other. You're old enough. What do you know about them?"

Vanessa shrugs. "Nada. They and the dragons were supposedly myths that the Daemoni rarely talked about." She looks over at Tristan and then Cam. "Did you ever hear anything about them?"

Emma calls for Cam from her room, so he leaves, and Tristan shakes his head. "Stuff of legends. Lucas once bragged about ending the dragons and 'all of their kind' when I was young, but I'd come to believe it was another of his lies. Nobody ever spoke of them outside of stories. If they were locked up in Hell all this time, then there was probably a reason for it, as far as Lucas and Satan were concerned. Sounds like the gargoyles were in the same boat."

"You okay with him here?" Vanessa asks Sheree.

"We can take him to Alexis's office." Tristan moves to grab the gargoyle.

Sheree steps in front of it. "No, it's okay. I'm fine. If he's been watching me and shifted, then he felt a level of comfort here, which might help bring him back again."

"Are you sure?" Tristan asks.

She nods emphatically. "I was surprised. Nothing more. Didn't mean to freak everyone out."

Tristan glares at the statue for a long moment, then nods and turns for the door. "Let me know as soon as he comes back. We need to learn everything about him and his kind. And whatever he knows about the dragons. In case we have new neighbors."

"Um . . . maybe he should have some time first," Sheree says. "To get used to everything. I can't imagine what he's going through."

Tristan looks over his shoulder at her, then at me. "If he knows anything that can help us, Sheree—"

He's cut off by the sound of loud alarms blaring through the bunker.

"I'll call you if he says anything when he comes back," Sheree yells over the blare.

Tristan nods then runs out the door, Vanessa right behind them. Owen's voice comes over the walkie-talkie on Sheree's hip.

"Water contamination. Over," he says.

"Those fookin' dragons. I know it is! If they're anywhere near here, they'll do whatever they can to drive ya off your own land!"

I spin around to find the gargoyle back in human shape, but only for a moment. He shudders and returns to stone.

CHAPTER 11

*W*hen I leave the Conversion Center, Tristan's already long gone. I find his mind signature near Owen's.

Do you need help? I ask him.

"*We're working on the pipes. Black magic's contaminating the water. We're trying to clear it out of our system.*"

I have only a vague understanding of what that even means. *Anything I can do?*

He hesitates, and I hold my breath the whole time I wait.

"*I'm sure Carlie could use some help,*" his mental voice snaps.

I frown and give him a mental ten-four before cutting off our connection and heading toward medical. Even more people than before fill the area and overflow into the hallway. She definitely needs help. She's filling cups with Owen's potion when I enter. "Here. Hand these out. It seems to be counteracting the poison in the water."

Everyone glares at me as I do, and I don't have to read their minds to feel their accusations. But I do anyway. And none of their thoughts are good. People are worried, many of them downright scared . . . and scary.

"*What the hell is she doing? She should be doing a lot more than handing out dirt-water. She's our leader for shit's sake!*"

"*If she can't lead us anymore, someone needs to.*"

"*They need to get us out of this mess, or we're all going to die.*"

"*We'll have to leave here soon. She promised us safety here, but she lied.*"

Most thoughts aren't clear sentences, though. Many are mostly

AGE OF ANGELS PART I: AWAKENED

emotions, while others are more visual. All, however, are just as full of despair. All seem to be upset with Alexis. With me.

Their growing desperation makes my heart hurt, but I don't know what to do about it. They're right. As their leader, I should be doing more than handing out cups of potion that may or may not help. But I'm practically useless.

"Anything else I can do?" I ask Carlie once everyone's received a dose of the potion.

"Not unless you magically remember going to med school."

"I went to med school?"

She sighs. "No. It was a joke. What I really need is trained doctors, but Tristan's the closest we have to that, and he's already stretched thin."

I frown with what feels like a subtle accusation. There's apparently nothing I can do here, and I can't stand all the critical stares, including from Carlie herself. So I leave medical, in search of some other way to help. I run into Tristan out in the hall.

"I don't think Carlie needs me anymore. I'm not much help in there."

"Because she needs *me*." The edge in his voice cuts even more sharply than before.

"Did you get the pipes fixed?"

"As best as we can for now, but we officially have no water source." He steps past me, reaching for the doorknob to the medical unit.

"Is there anything else I can do?" I nearly beg.

He squints at me. "Did you read all of the reports Robin brought by?"

I sigh. "Yeah, I finished yesterday, remember? But I don't exactly know what to do about the skirmishes. What to tell them. I need some help with that."

A low growl of frustration emanates from his throat. "Of course you do. I don't know why you're even . . ." He stops whatever thought he has and lets out another irritated sigh. "No, there's nothing you can help with, Alexis, except to get your damn memories back. I need my wife. The twins need their mother. And these people need their leader!"

His voice rises so loud by the end, I'm sure the entire Loft hears him, especially since half the residents are supernaturals. He throws open the door to medical and stomps in, slamming it shut behind him. I stand in the hallway, staring at the vibrating slab of wood and feeling the stares of those in the corridor with me. Any secret about my condition has been blown. Their thoughts flood into my mind, and now they're more worried than ever. And more leery of me. *Yay. Way to go, Tristan.*

I hurry away, although I don't know where to go. I end up at the nursery where the babies are with Teal and Teah. Teah scurries to the door when she sees me.

"They just went down for a nap," she whispers. "You probably don't want to wake them."

I crane my neck to look over her shoulder, but she's taller than me, so I peek around her arm. The twins are sleeping soundly in two cribs. I nod and turn away, blinking against the sting in my eyes. I can't even do anything for Brielle and Elliana, the two most helpless souls in this place. Besides me.

As the afternoon grows into evening, panic begins to manifest in The Loft. Word about my amnesia spreads at the same time more people fall ill from the poisoned water. Tristan calls together what he refers to as a core council meeting—a gathering in the conference room outside my office that includes the usual people around us. Vanessa, Owen, Blossom, Jax, Sheree, and Carlie sit at the tables, and they all discuss plans for the mission the next day. I sit in my office with the door open, listening to them, but not an actual part of the meeting. There isn't much I have to offer, and my own plans form in my mind.

"The sooner we can make sure the water's safe and hook up to it, the better," Tristan says as they all stand up. I peek out at them to find him flicking a glance my way. "And if you happen to notice anything that could have messed up Alexis, even better."

He follows everyone out of the room without a word to me. I decide it would be best to steer clear of him the rest of the evening, so I stay in my office, not even going back for bed. If he can't stand to be in the same room with me during the day, he surely wouldn't want to be in the same bed.

I stay at my desk and skim through the books I'd supposedly written, thinking about the highlighted parts. I wonder what they all mean, what their significance is, when my mind drifts. I let it go, skimming over the mind signatures again, picking out the ones I'd come to identify. Someone's thoughts, though, someone I'm not familiar with, draws me in, almost as though I've entered a trance. Or a dream.

As though I'm witnessing it myself, as though I'm right there, I find myself in the middle of a battle. Terror fills me as I survey the area, listening to the clanks of weapons slamming into each other and the screams of the injured and dying while counting what appears to be hundreds of bodies scattered on the snow stained with black, silver, and red. Grief fills me as I crawl to one of the bloody and battered bodies and gather it into my arms. I look around again through tear-filled eyes and scream for help. Help that never comes.

I awake, or come back, or whatever with a start, blinking several times as I realize I'm still in my office. In the distance, in the residential area, someone screams in their sleep. And I know, that was not a dream invented by imagination, but a real-life memory brought forth by someone's subconscious. Somebody in a great deal of emotional pain. My heart grows heavy.

Wondering how many others suffer like this, I peruse other minds. Every single mind I enter hurts in some way. I see varying memories of that same battle, but also scenes of bombs dropping, cars exploding, and entire cities burning. I witness mushroom clouds rise over various horizons and people scrambling for safety. Before my mind's eye, supernaturals attack norms in cities that still stand, killing them in the streets as they drink their blood or tear apart their flesh. What appears to be dead corpses gnaw mindlessly on other humans. People gun down other people, fighting over food and water.

Now I understand why Tristan had said he wishes I don't have to remember all of this. Not only because they're terrible memories in and of themselves, but because in every case, these survivors had been praying for help, for someone to save and protect them. Some of them specifically begged for Alexis's help or clung to hope and *promises* that she would protect the world. But she hadn't.

I hadn't.

Although I can't remember why it would have been my responsibility to protect these people, to save the world, they nonetheless had expected it from me. Their accusing eyes earlier now make even more sense. Tristan is wrong. They don't look up to me to lead them. They don't believe what the Angels have told them, whatever that means. They think of me as a big disappointment. A failure.

CHAPTER 12

*W*hen I hear the babies start crying for their middle-of-the-night feeding, I'm glad I'd brought the pump to the kitchen earlier so I wouldn't have to face Tristan now. He'd been working frantically all day on things I should have been doing, and my very presence is a trigger for his anger. So I pump in a shower stall in the communal bathroom, then take the bottles to the kitchen. I'm surprised to find Blossom here, dressed in a hoodie and yoga pants.

"Oh, I'll take those," she says. She holds a couple of other bottles in her hands. "I couldn't sleep, so I may as well work."

I don't hand her the bottles. "What do you mean? The babies must have already eaten. They're asleep. They'll need these for later."

"Oh, no! You didn't think we actually fed them your milk right now, did you?"

I cock my head.

"Not when we don't know what kind of magic mind-jacked you. It could be anywhere in your system," she continues. "I need to test these. I should probably take some more of your blood, too. What we found tonight—" She glances at a wall clock that shows a little before four o'clock in the morning. "Last night, I guess, well, it's nothing we've seen before. We need to break it down and figure it out, or we'll never get you cured."

Which is probably just as well, from what I've seen. I don't need to know anymore. I only need to prepare.

"So what are the babies eating then?" I ask.

"You had some milk stored up. You often produce more than they can eat, just like you do everything more than everyone else, so we had some stocked up. Good thing, too, considering. But unfortunately, it's about gone, and I don't know what we're going to do—"

I cut her off, because she seems to have a habit of babbling on various subjects at once. "Wait. The milk's almost gone? How much is left?"

She turns back toward the fridge and peeks inside. "Based on what you said the other day about how much they're eating now, there's enough for another day, but that's it."

"That's *it*? And then what?"

"Well, the scouts scavenged some baby formula before you had the babies, just in case it was ever needed, but there's not much of that, either. And that needs water, although we might be okay in that regard if the samples the team brings back tomorrow prove to be as clean as the first ones. Hopefully, they *will* come back again, since they did last time. The problem is then getting our system connected to it, which will take magic and probably a day or so, out there where that dragon or whatever that beast you saw is that seems to be driving everyone off—"

"Dragon," I say, lost in thought. Had what we'd seen out there really been a dragon? I hadn't caught a good enough look to know for sure, but it *had* shot fire down on us. "There's been a lot of talk about them, but I don't feel like I know them. I mean, I knew vampires and others existed, but I don't remember that about dragons. I don't remember gargoyles, either, but that guy blames the dragons for everything. Maybe they could have caused this, too?"

I twirl my finger around my temple.

Blossom's brows pinch together as she stares at the ground. She speaks slowly for once. "Neither have been in our world for centuries—that we knew of, anyway. The faeries released the dragons from Hell. At least, that's what we'd heard from our people in other parts of the world who have seen the beasts, too. But, anyway, I don't think they could have . . ." She pauses without me having to interrupt her, and then she finally looks up at me with a glint in her eye. Her voice picks up again. "Owen said the dragon came after you woke up, but there's something else it could have done before you even arrived. Maybe set a trap or something. Or, my Aunt Sylvie used to be infatuated with the legends, and she always thought the dragons were still around, but invisible. Said they could cloak themselves.

There could be truth to that, too, and they decided to come out of hiding now that the world's different. Or who knows what else? I mean, we really know nothing about—"

"Blossom," I interrupt again. She clamps her mouth shut. "The point?"

"I'm saying Owen could be wrong. It *could* be the dragon. We'll have to find out, won't we? Besides the water, this is the first real idea we've had!" The glint disappears, taking the excitement with it. She frowns. "Since we don't know their magic, we'll need something from the dragon to test and compare. Some part of it, like scales. Do they have scales? Or blood would work, too. I wonder how hard that would be to get. And I need to start work on this immediately to try to isolate the magic in you so I can compare as soon as they get back tomorrow. Can I get some of that blood?"

I agree to give her what she needs, because that seems to be something Alexis would do, but I don't hold on to hope that they'll be able to cure me. In fact, it's better for everyone if they don't. When we're done, I find myself in the same place where I'd spent my first night here—on the steps to our compartment.

"I thought I'd told you no more sleeping on the steps." Tristan's voice comes from behind me only a few short minutes after I sit down.

I turn to look up at him. He pulls a shirt down over his muscular torso of perfection as he trots down the stairs. I have to swallow down the lump in my throat.

"I, uh, wasn't sleeping," I manage to say. "Can't sleep."

"Me neither." He sits down next to me, but stares straight ahead. "Listen. I'm sorry about how I treated you earlier."

"No biggie. There's a lot going on, and I'm of absolutely no help."

He rests his elbows on his knees and folds his hands together as he blows out a breath. "Yeah, there is, but it's no excuse for my behavior. You can't help it."

He's right. But there's something I can do to make his life easier and help everyone here in The Loft. I just have to figure out how to execute, and do so soon, before the group leaves for the lake later this morning.

"Can I ask you a question?" I ask.

One side of his mouth lifts up, and his voice comes out with a teasing lilt to it. "You can always ask."

I feel like he means something by the reply, but don't know what. "The flying thing—have we always been able to do that? I've been trying to figure out how I know all my words and how to walk and even fight, but not how to fly."

His voice drops, the teasing tone gone. "It's a new thing. We've only had the wings for a little over a year, when the Angels decided to start this new era on Earth."

"Ah. I guess that explains it." I pause. "Do you, uh, think you could teach me how to fly again?"

He looks at me with raised eyebrows. "Right now?"

"Is it a bad time? You probably want to go back to sleep—"

"No. I wouldn't be able to anyway." He glances up at the door then turns back to me. "Sure, why not? Everyone's still asleep, and it's a good stress reliever."

"I think we can both use that." I offer a smile.

"Be right back." He disappears for a moment, then returns, handing the dagger and a knife to me. "We never go out without weapons."

"The twins will be okay?" I ask as we walk up the tunnel toward the outside doors.

"Vanessa doesn't really sleep. She'll take care of them if they wake up. We won't be gone long, though. We need to be back before the team leaves."

He pushes the button to raise the first overhead door, and we duck underneath it. In a moment, we're swallowed by pitch darkness, which is good because it hides my expression. I don't want to give away my plan yet, because he might make us turn around and go back. In another moment, the outside door lifts. As we pass under it, I feel a tug at my heart and soul—a tug toward Brielle and Ellianna. I swallow against the tightening in my throat and shove the feeling away.

"Wings out," Tristan says, and I stare at him blankly. "You only have to think it."

Oh, right. As soon as I think it, my wings appear. He launches into the air and shows me how to use my muscles to control the wings and fly. It's easier than I expected. I suppose some part of me still knew after all. I must have been too surprised by the wings before to remember how to use them.

Flying together in the pre-dawn darkness is peaceful and . . . romantic. We don't stray far from The Loft compound, but fly wide circles around it, skimming over the treetops. Without the harsh light of the sun on the grayness of the world, the landscape below looks quite normal, if seeing it from a hundred feet in the air is normal. You can almost believe there is hope for this world.

When I see a square patch of ground that looks different from the rest, I drop down. I stumble with the terrible landing, catching myself on the fence that surrounds an acre or so of land. The grass appears as though it may have actually been green, and trees with real leaves dot the space.

"Your blood cleaned out the black magic here," Tristan says, his voice quiet and filled with reverence as he lands next to me—perfectly graceful, of course. "The mages keep it growing year-round. We planted a tree in tribute for each of our loved ones who died in the Battle of Armageddon."

A wooden sign hangs from rope on each tree with a name and portrait painted on each one. Names and faces I should probably recognize. At the base of each trunk and tied to the low limbs, people have left little trinkets in memory. My heart shrinks and grows heavy, as though my blood has turned to lead. I press my hand to my chest, trying to push away the rising sob. These are the people who'd died under my leadership. The people who'd been part of The Loft's family.

"They're all dead because of you."

I startle and spin around at the unfamiliar voice, although it came in my head, not my ears. I don't recognize it and find no mind signature nearby. Someone from The Loft must have had as hard of a time sleeping as Tristan and me. Who can blame them? They all suffer from PTSD and tragedy.

I wipe my cheek against my shoulder, then spring back into the air. We fly in silence for a long time, until I feel like I can breathe again. Then Tristan lands in the top branches of a tall, thick tree and gestures for me to join him. I manage to perch myself onto the branch next to his. Not feeling as steady as him, I lean against the trunk. Below us spreads a wide pit that appears to have been a lake at one time. Dark water pools in its bottom, not nearly as deep as it should be. It must be the water source The Loft has been using until now.

"We haven't been able to fly together like this in a long time," Tristan says, his voice soft and buttery. "I miss it."

"We used to do this a lot?"

His head twitches in a slight shake. "Not a lot. There's always something going on, especially with the babies. But sometimes, we just need to get out, away from everyone else."

Ah. I understand. To be alone. I wonder if he thinks that's why I've asked him to do this for me. Is that why he'd agreed so easily? As he leans in toward me, his beautiful hazel eyes intensely on mine, I think it's exactly why. The love Carlie had spoken about has been missing the last couple of days, but it shines clearly in his gaze now, piercing into me and making me want it more than life itself. The look in his eyes heats into one of desire, and I can't help but remember the feeling of his erection pressed into my back. In immediate response, my heart bursts into a gallop, and electricity zings through my body. I return his hungry stare, my mouth parted already, needing to feel his lips on mine. His hand lifts to my face, and I press my cheek into his palm. His thumb caresses my lips as he leans closer, and my tongue slides over my bottom lip to meet it. But tasting isn't enough. I suck it into my mouth, and the look on his face makes my whole body explode with heat.

Both of his hands grip my face now, and he pulls me closer. Our lips crash together, finally giving me what I've wanted since that first kiss. And so much more. Our mouths part, and our tongues meet each other in a desperate dance. The delicious taste of mangos and papayas, sage, and lime fill my mouth, and I nip and suck hungrily. He returns the gestures, as though trying to devour me, sending a web of electricity over my scalp and throughout my body. His hand slides down, over my neck and down my back, pulling me over to his branch. He hitches my leg up over his hip, eliminating all space between us so my whole body presses against his powerful one. My breasts swell until they ache, and my hard nipples poke through the thin fabric of my top and rub against his chest. Electricity jolts from the tips to my groin, and I grind my pelvis against the hard ridge growing between us. When his hand slides under my top and caresses its way slowly up my ribs, I think I might die. Or maybe I already have and this is heaven.

His hands return to my face and gently push me back, breaking the kiss so we can take a breath. His eyes lock on mine, gold flecks glinting in the emerald irises. My body screams, *kiss me, kiss me, kiss me, more, more, more*. At the same time, though, my mind yells, *no, no, no, don't get attached!* He continues to stare at me as his brows dip downward. He drops his hands away, and his gaze slides over my face, down to my lips and back up. His mouth turns down, sadness filling his eyes. I lean in, wanting to make that look disappear, but he shakes his head.

"You're not her," he says. "I feel like it'd be cheating."

Before I can reply, he launches himself into the air. My heart breaks and sinks at the same time, hurting for him, for what I've done to him. What I've done to all of them. I look and sound like his wife, like their friend and their leader, but I'm an impostor. If my mind hasn't already been made up about what I need to do, it is now.

I fly after him, staying a good hundred yards behind him. When we approach the door of The Loft, Owen, Vanessa, and the rest of the team are exiting out of it, preparing to leave on their mission. The two norms who'd been with us last time are on motorcycles, and everyone's armed heavier than they'd been before. Owen magically directs four large, square, plastic containers in front of him. Filled, they'll hold several days' worth of drinking water for everyone. Enough to last until they can permanently tap into the lake.

Tristan drops down in front of them, but I take my time in joining them as I try to figure out my angle. Okay, and maybe recover from what just happened between us. I hang in the air, barely in range, as a few of his words float up to me. ". . . can't stay . . . better off without her . . . permanent solution." I suck my bottom lip between my teeth as my heart jolts in my chest. Is he talking about me? He must be. He's an intelligent guy, and he must have come to the same conclusion I have. Of course, he could mean something else, and I could read his mind to know, but it doesn't matter. The words are still true. And what if there's no cure? What if they never discover an antidote and my memories remain forever locked away? There's a very good possibility I'd never be the Alexis he wants and needs. I'll always be a charlatan. Decision made, I take a deep breath, swallow down my emotions, and drop to the ground to join them.

"We have to harvest some dragon blood," Owen is saying to Tristan as I touch down in front of them. "Alexis and Blossom had some ideas last night."

Tristan looks over at me with accusation in his eyes, probably because I hadn't told him about it. I shrug. "It's an idea, right?"

"Aidan swears the dragons have done everything, trying to drive us away," Sheree says. "So it's likely."

"If we can trust him," Tristan mutters.

"We can." Sheree's words come with full confidence. I check her mind and learn she already has some pretty strong feelings for the gargoyle. *Huh. Interesting.*

Tristan scrubs a hand over his face before nodding. "Then I should go with you. We need someone who can fly. Cam's left and won't be back for a couple of days."

He's making this easier than I expected.

"You need to stay," Owen says. "You're still Omega Team, remember? The ones who stay behind to keep everyone calm. The people need you more than ever, as bad as everything's getting in there. The antidote cured the illness, but people are dehydrated. Some of the kids severely. Carlie needs you."

Tristan growls. "You need help, though."

Owen's eyes slide over toward me. Wow. They're all making this easier.

"No!" Tristan snaps. "That's the last thing we need."

Wow. Jerk much?

"They need my help," I say. "I can do this. It's finally something I *can* do."

"Absolutely not," Tristan says, his tone final.

"Then you'll just have to trust us," Vanessa chimes, though the sweet musical quality drips with ice. She glances up at the lightening sky. "We need to go."

They say their goodbyes, then run down the gravel drive after the motorcycles. After they disappear from sight, Tristan walks inside the first door of The Loft and waits for me to follow him. As the door begins to close, though, I run back outside.

I'm going with them, I tell him as I launch myself in the air.

"*The hell you are!*"

The hell I'm not! You have no say over me, and I need to do this. I need to go back to where this all started. Maybe I'll remember. Or maybe I can at least help them with the dragon. You said it yourself. And then maybe you can get your Alexis back.

"*Lexi!*" he bellows at me, but he doesn't follow me. He doesn't try to stop me, although I know he could have. Perhaps if he knew my real plan, he would have. Or maybe not. "*You planned this all along, didn't you?*" When I don't answer him, he lets out a mental sigh. "*Use your mind to call for me if you need help.*"

CHAPTER 13

*R*ather than flying ahead of the team this time, as they said I had last time, I stay right over them, while keeping my mind open for other mind signatures. They hope we'll find the other scouting groups who'd gone out before us and might have been wandering the area aimlessly because they don't remember anything. I also search for the dragon. We reach the lake an hour or so later with no sign from the flying, fire-emitting beast. While the team collects their water samples, I circle the lake twice, but find nobody else.

Shit. If we don't find the dragon soon, I'll run out of time and opportunity.

Commotion breaks out below me. A couple of surprised shouts are followed by everyone yelling at each other about an attack as they all jump to attention. Owen gives orders as he rubs his hands together, then throws them upward toward me. Air swooshes around me, and my ears pop. Vanessa darts through the woods. Sheree bursts into a tiger and takes off running, too. One of the norms raises a gun and the other a crossbow as they turn in circles. Owen looks through the tree branches up at me and taps on his temple. I think it means he wants to mind-talk. I hesitate, thinking this might be my chance, but as something swishes through the air by them, I know I can't leave them like this.

"*Alexis, come in,*" Owen's saying in his mind when I tap into it.

I'm in, I reply with a snort.

"*What is it?*" he asks. When I don't answer, he clarifies, "*What's attacking us?*"

I have no idea. I don't sense anything. There aren't any other mind signatures around.

"*Faeries, then?*" Again, he explains when I don't reply. "*You can't hear faeries' thoughts.*"

Huh. I can't read *everyone's* thoughts? I wonder if that means I can't read the dragon's either. And if Blossom's aunt is right about the invisibility, the thing could be anywhere around, and we wouldn't know it.

"There it is again," one of the norms shouts as he spins, trying to aim his crossbow on something that's no more than a blur. It disappears. "What is that?"

"Too tiny to be the beast we saw the other day." I descend to look closer. Pink and yellow dust settles over his head and around him, as though an invisible bubble surrounds him.

"I have you shielded," Owen says. "Whatever that was tried to throw this at you. Don't move."

Owen pulls a jar out of his bag and with a twitch of his fingers, flicks the dust into the container. While he's putting the jar away, Vanessa and Sheree, in tiger form, return. Vanessa holds what appears at first glance to be a small child in one hand, except she has a mature face, and I can't find a mind signature attached to it. Is this a faerie? I drop to the ground, pulling my wings in tight behind me.

"I think we have our culprit," Vanessa says, dangling the creature by its collar.

She looks like what I'd imagine a faerie to look like—small, pointy ears, up-tilted eyes, a delicate but pointy nose and chin, and lime green hair pulled into a ponytail that starts at the top of her head and ends near her butt. She wears what looks to be fighting leathers like ours, but hot pink instead of black and so form-fitting, I can't be one hundred percent sure it's not her skin. She has no wings, but I assume the miniature sized crossbow dangling from one of Vanessa's fingers belongs to her. She glares at us with oversized eyes the same bright green as her hair as she kicks and squirms in Vanessa's grip.

"What are you?" Owen asks, a mixture of anger and awe filling his voice as he leans down to inspect her more closely. Hmm. Does that mean this isn't a faerie?

The creature sticks out her tongue and blows a raspberry. Pink and yellow dust flies, settling on the invisible shields Owen has around us. With an indignant harrumph, she falls still, crosses her arms over her chest, and sticks her full bottom lip out in a pout.

"Looks like the same stuff we saw on the ground the other day," Vanessa says. "What Sheree thought was pollen."

The tiger hums in agreement. I'd noticed it, too, and had also thought it to be some kind of pollen.

"Are you a pixie?" Owen asks, and the creature lifts her chin and looks away from him.

"Huh. Haven't seen one of them since I was little," Vanessa says. "A couple hundred years ago."

"Another creature the faeries released from Hell," I surmise.

Everyone looks at me with almost as much surprise as they'd been looking at the pixie.

"You remember?" Vanessa asks.

I press my lips together and glance at the pixie. I don't think it smart to reveal our problems to what might be a foe.

No, I silently answer. *You guys said the dragon had been released by the faeries, so it was an assumption.*

"Of course she doesn't," a squeaky little voice says. "She won't until—"

The pixie cuts herself off.

Vanessa gives her a shake. "Until what? What did you do to her?"

The creature's lips remain sealed shut. She admitted to nothing, but she doesn't deny it, either. Has my memory loss really been her doing and not the dragon's?

"Are there more of you?" Vanessa demands. The pixie lifts her chin in defiance. "You couldn't have possibly attacked us by yourself."

"I so could have!" The pixie squeaks as she stomps her little foot. "And I did a fine job at it, too. They weren't sure that I could, but I did."

Everyone's heads cock at the same time.

"Who?" Vanessa asks. "Who's *they*? Who are you working for?"

The pixie's breath catches as guilt passes over her face—she's said too much. She presses her lips together and turns away, her chin lifted again.

"You do know it's because of Alexis that you're even free, don't you?" Owen asks. I turn my head toward him and lift a brow. Something else to blame on me? "Because of her, the faeries were able to escape. None of you would have been freed from Satan's capture if she hadn't done what she did."

He says this as though it's a good thing, veneration filling his voice. I suppose being freed from Satan and Hell are a good thing for the creatures who'd been captured, but based on what we've seen so far—a beast that's likely a dragon breathing fire-bombs on us and this ornery little imp—I don't think it's such a good thing for the world. The pixie doesn't fully understand, either. Her brows pinch together as she regards me from the corner of her slanted eye. When I catch her gaze, she immediately looks away, lifts her nose higher, and lets out another little harrumph.

"You owe her your life," Vanessa adds, but the pixie pretends not to hear, although both the tips of her ears and her lips twitch.

Owen blows out a breath. "Let's get her back to The Loft. I'll bind her up, and Vanessa, you're in charge of her. We'll find a way to make her talk there. Sheree and Alexis, watch for the dragon. The rest of you, fill up the jugs. I'll do the vats."

With a twirl of his hand, the pixie's arms fall and are pinned to her sides by something invisible. She tries to open her mouth to protest, but she's apparently gagged, too. Pink and yellow dust plume from her flared nostrils.

Everyone goes to work. Owen takes a wider stance, moves his arms and upper torso toward the lake, and then leans back as though pulling on an invisible rope. A stream of water rises into the air and falls into the opening of one of the large plastic containers. At the same time as I bend my legs to spring upward, a shadow falls over us, and fire rains down, encircling us. The norms yell profanities as they jump out of the way. Owen redirects the water to extinguish the flames.

Vanessa gives the pixie another shake. "Is that who you're working with? The dragon?"

The pixie glances upward, pulls her bottom lip in, and lifts her shoulder in a shrug. I don't wait to see Vanessa's reaction. She can handle the pixie. I need to deal with this dragon, if that's what this beast really is.

I spring up and soar into the air. As soon as I burst through the treetops, I gasp. No longer seeing only its underbelly, but now the creature in full, I can hardly believe my eyes. The beast, with skin and scales in various shades of teal and blue, is a beautiful sight to behold. Wings bigger than a ship's sails spread out at least twenty or thirty feet from a body four times the size of a Clydesdale horse. Its long tail swishes back and forth in sharp arcs as it flies away from me. Definitely a dragon. Artists of the myths got this one right, although its beauty could never be fully captured with colored pencils or paints.

"*LEAVE.*" The deep, beastly voice booms in my head like thunder.

Guess that answers my question.

I fly after it. I'll get this done for Blossom because I like her, and I want to help her solve this problem in case it happens again. But then I'll be off and away.

The dragon's head whips around, and its bright blue eye finds me. Another blast of fire surges out of its mouth. I lift up to avoid it, but realize the flames wouldn't have hit me anyway. Owen's shield around me would have blocked the fire, but I think the dragon might have missed me on purpose.

"*LEAVE,*" it booms again, the sound rocking my brain.

Not until I get what we need.

During our sparring match, Vanessa had told me about the electrical power I harbor, so I try to shoot a current at the dragon. I think it snickers in my mind as it shoots forward in the sky, unaffected by my attack as it soars away from me. I fly after it and try again, doubting my little dagger would do anything to this beast, but determined to bring it down.

"*Alexis,*" Owen calls out to me. "*Don't try to fight it alone.*"

Then come help me! I give my wings a couple of hard flaps to catch up with the dragon, trying to figure out how I can wrestle it to the ground. I at least need to get it closer to Owen. I develop a plan that's half-assed and stupid, but I'm at a loss for any other ideas.

I pull my dagger from its sheath and fly harder for the beast as it heads for the hills on the far side of the lake. At the same time, I try to read its thoughts, but they're difficult to grasp, like Sheree's when she shifts into her tiger form. Once I'm alongside it where its tail meets its body, I slash my dagger outward, into the dragon's hide. It lets out an ear-piercing shriek, and I jerk the blade free, then fly away, hoping the creature will follow me. I feel a blast of heat, but nothing else. I turn in the air. The dragon continues across the lake in a purposeful flight, and I look toward where he's heading. Rising above the hills behind the far shore is another, slightly smaller dragon, and this one colored in teals and purples, rather than blues. A thought-image pops into my mind from her; something about eggs. Then my breath catches and someone swears a string of profanities in my head as more dragons rise from the hills—half a dozen now, all of them in vibrant colors and terrifyingly magnificent.

"*Let's get out of here,*" Owen calls to me again. "*We can't take all of them on, and we already have what we need.*"

I stare at the beautiful creatures for a moment longer, and then look down at my dagger. Blue blood drips from the blade. It will have to be enough because Owen's right—I can't even take the one down, let alone six.

I got some of its blood, I tell Owen. *But nothing else.*

"*That might help, but I don't think we'll need it. I think this pixie's what we need. Come on. Let's get you back and get you fixed up.*"

I hang in the air, hesitating. This might be my only chance. A couple of the dragons begin flying my way. *Shit.* I swing around, surveying the area as I do, trying to decide the best direction to disappear while keeping one eye on the slowly approaching dragons. What are they up to? Why aren't they attacking? They must know they have the advantage. And from what the gargoyle had said, they would have no qualms with killing us. So I'm definitely not heading in their direction, which is straight north. The Loft sits to the east, so that means going west or south. If I could only remember exactly where we are and what, if anything, remains in either direction.

"*Don't you dare!*" Vanessa yells in my head, startling me out of my thoughts.

Dare what? I try to sound innocent as I move in their direction. I haven't been sharing my thoughts again, have I? The dragons slow their own flight.

"*I know you. I've seen the look in your eyes. I smell it on you. That whole impostor syndrome bullshit you get.*"

I pull back, hovering in midair over the lake. *But I* am *an impostor.*

She stands on the shore, her hands on her hips, the pixie dangling from one and the bow from the other, as she glares up at me. "*Yeah, you're a little fucked up in the head right now, but we're going to get you fixed. And then you're going to get over yourself and do what everyone expects and needs from you.*"

Which is?

"*Lead them, you idiot. They need you!*"

I roll my eyes. *Not from what I've seen. They'll be better off without me. All of you will be.*

I don't say it in a pitiful, woe-is-me kind of way. I don't have those kinds of feelings, because I don't have any emotional attachment. Well . . .

not much anyway. I state what I know as fact. Even if the evidence doesn't point to less than stellar results of my leadership skills, the feelings of the people toward me does. They'll never follow someone they don't believe in.

"*You're damn lucky I can't fly,*" Vanessa growls, "*because I'd so be kicking your ass right now.*"

"*You don't have to,*" Owen pipes in. "*I got this.*"

Get out of my freaking head! I yell at the same time I'm dragged through the air toward the shore against my will, as though I'm a kite on a string, being reeled in.

"Get your shit together, and you can block us out any time you want to," Vanessa says aloud when my feet hit the ground.

Owen's hands are directed at me, keeping some kind of magical pressure on my body that's different than Tristan's paralyzing power, but nearly as strong. And equally as effective.

"You're going to keep me prisoner like her?" I sneer as my gaze darts toward the pixie.

"Are you a flight risk like she is?" Owen countes. I don't reply. "That's what I thought. You're coming back with us, and we're going to get you fixed. Then at least you can make an *informed* decision whether you want to take off or not."

Dark shadows pass over us from above as the dragons circle us. They still don't attack, but it's only a matter of time. I've probably made things worse by drawing first blood, and now the people of The Loft could be in even more danger. Because of me. Great. I'm a hazard to them, but I can't abandon them now. And Owen has a point—before I make the decision to take off, I really should be more informed.

"Okay, fine," I concede. "I'll go back with you. For now."

CHAPTER 14

Owen lets out a breath and flicks his fingers toward me. I'm set free from the invisible bindings holding me in place.

"I'll make a portal," he says. "We don't want those dragons following us back on foot."

"We might not make it back," one of the norms says as he eyes the sky, his head crouched down between his shoulders as though ducking might save him from the fiery beasts.

"What's a portal? And why don't we do that flashing thing?" I ask. "Can they follow that?"

"Possibly," Vanessa says. "If they have any flashing ability and are close enough to follow our trails."

"It's not an option. These vats are too big and heavy to take in a flash," Owen says. His eyebrows squeeze together, forming three lines between them, as he seems to concentrate. "We have to portal it."

I have no choice but to take their word for it. There's so much I still don't know or understand, even about myself. I sure hope they can bring my memories back because I don't want to have to stick around long enough to learn it all.

Owen twirls his hands in the air in front of him, squeezes them together, and then pulls them apart as though tearing through a covering. A rent in the air appears—that's the only way to explain it. It's as though he's actually torn a hole in the space-time continuum. Beyond it, in that space of air before me, I can see the door to The Loft, shimmering as though it's not quite there. All around the image are the woods we stand in. Sheree passes through the hole first, ending up near The Loft's door. The norms follow, and then Owen magically lifts the vats of water.

"After you," he says.

I hesitate long enough for Vanessa to come up behind me, her breath on my neck. Before she can push me through, I step into the hole. The air immediately changes, although the difference in the smell and taste of the air and in the sounds around us compared to the woods by the lake is minimal. The shadows from the nearby trees fall a little differently. Other than that, there's nothing to tell me I've covered fifty miles with one step. I turn to watch Vanessa come through with the pixie squirming and protesting as she does. Owen magically lifts the vats of water and directs them through as he follows. He closes up the portal as soon as he passes to this side of it.

"They probably already know where we are, but maybe that will give us a little extra time," he says.

"If they know where The Loft is, though, why haven't they already attacked?" I wonder aloud.

"Good question."

The pixie swinging from Vanessa's hand lets out a little squeak, but when we look at her, she turns her head away again, her lips pressed tightly together. I can't read her thoughts, but I have to wonder if she knows something that can help us, but refuses to share it. What have those dragons promised her? It must be something worthy for her to be so loyal.

"Are pixies and dragons usually allies?" I ask. I don't expect an answer from the green-haired pipsqueak, but maybe the others know.

"Who the hell knows?" Vanessa quips. "They're a type of fae, and fae do what they want with whomever they want. The dragons must owe this one a big-time favor, and if not, they will. That's the only way faeries do anything. Their tit for tat isn't exactly equal."

"Ha!" the pixie squeaks. "The dragons won't do anything for anybody. They owe nobody, not even you, princess. Or queen, I guess you are now. They don't care who freed them. They only care about themselves and their precious treasures."

Vanessa lifts the little thing up to eye level. "Then why are you working with them? Why were you helping them drive us away?"

The pixie must realize too late that she's said more than she wanted to. She narrows her lime green eyes, scrunches her face up, and sticks her tongue out, about to blow another raspberry. But Vanessa's quicker. Her fangs drop, and she draws the creature closer to her mouth. The pixie's eyes grow wide, and she sucks her tongue back in.

"What I wouldn't do for faerie blood." Vanessa's words are a hiss full of desire and hunger.

"You wouldn't!" the pixie declares. "The dust—"

"I'd deal with it for the high." Vanessa's tongue slides over the tip of a fang, then she pulls the sharp, elongated teeth back into her gums. "Blossom will start working on an antidote to your dust as soon as we're inside, now that we know. The poison would be out of my system right after the high wore off. *Totally* worth it."

The pixie glares back wordlessly, and I stare at Vanessa, too. I don't know whether to take the vampire seriously or not, and it appears as though the pixie doesn't, either.

Hoping she feels the threat, I press her with more questions. "If you're not working for the dragons, then who are you working for?"

The pixie's glare shoots toward me, and her eyes widen for the briefest of moments. I've taken a guess, but she pretty much confirms my theory. Her eyes flick away as she lifts her chin once again.

"Who says I'm not working with the dragons?" she asks haughtily.

"The fae don't work for free," Owen mutters.

"And if dragons don't pay—" Sheree starts.

"I said they don't *owe*."

"So they *are* paying you?" I ask. "Or . . . they've enslaved you?"

"Ha! They wish!"

"What are they paying you then?" Vanessa asks. "Maybe we'll pay more."

The pixie seems to consider this for a moment, but then she smirks. "I'm bound by secrecy. Make me an offer I can't refuse, but know this: before you can change my loyalty, you must know whom I'm loyal to."

"So it's not the dragons?" I guess, but she falls silent again and refuses to answer any more questions we throw her way. "For shit's sake! Are the fae always so maddening?"

"Yes," everyone answers in unison.

Tristan and Blossom meet us right inside the doors. I avoid looking at him, afraid to see disappointment in his eyes or expression because I've returned. *It's only temporary*, I tell myself since I can't tell him. I don't know why he'd try to stop me from leaving, but everyone else has, so it's possible. I just need to keep my plans to myself.

Owen and Blossom disappear with the water and the pixie dust, while the rest of the council meet in the conference room to discuss what to do about the dragons. Aidan insists the only solution is to fight them.

"They will not hesitate in attacking until they drive you completely out and away," he says. He looks at me. "You mentioned eggs?"

I nod. He snorts.

"Then I am wrong. They will not drive you away. They will simply kill you. Us. Everyone here. Their eggs are more valuable than gold . . . which they also likely have hidden."

"We don't want their eggs," Sheree says.

"Or their gold," I say.

"It matters none."

"We can fight them," Tristan says. He looks at me with a glint in his eye. "Show them who's in charge."

I immediately look away. *Yeah, right.* That certainly isn't me in charge. Maybe he means himself. He's trying to tell me he agrees with me. Good. That would only make things easier.

Tristan hounds the gargoyle about the dragons' weaknesses, and then they all discuss strategy. Blossom comes charging in during the discussion, sometime in the late afternoon.

She holds out a cup to me. "Try this."

Ignoring the strange smell, I swallow down the clear contents. Everyone has fallen silent, and all eyes lock on me with expectation. Nothing happens. Mumbling something under her breath, Blossom leaves for another try, and the others go back to their conversation. Tristan looks at me several times, as though asking for my input, but I really know nothing about planning a battle, offensive and defensive tactics, and the like. I'm probably supposed to know, but my memory is limited to self-defense, and that's more on an instinctual level. When they break for a late supper, I decide to join Blossom to see how she's coming along.

I find her in the little lab, no Owen around, and the pixie sitting on the workbench, apparently still magically bound. I sit in the corner and try each new batch Blossom creates, tweaked just a little bit from the previous one.

"Ugh! I have no idea what the problem is!" She sinks into a wooden chair next to the workbench and drops her head into her hands. Her long, dirty-blonde hair hangs in curtains around her. I feel her frustration, but don't know what to say. Maybe this is hopeless, but saying so probably wouldn't help. She finally lifts her head, crosses her arms over her ample chest, and glares at the pixie. "What aren't you telling me, you little imp?"

The pixie mirrors her position, but says nothing.

"I'm going to throttle her!" Blossom's voice booms, angrier than I've heard it yet as she springs to her feet and stomps out of the room.

I follow her out. "Are you out of options?"

She spins on me and throws her arms in the air. "There's some piece of information we're missing because of that obstinate little twit. The ingredients are there, but the magic isn't right."

Tristan's voice booms in my mind. "*Alexis, meet us in the conference room. Bring Blossom!*"

The urgency in his voice worries me. "Come on."

Blossom follows me as we hustle toward the front of The Loft. Owen and Tristan are jogging down the tunnel from the front doors. We enter the conference room to find Sheree, Jax, and Carlie returned from dinner.

"We have a big problem," Owen announces once we're all in the room. "I felt something approaching our wards, so Tristan and I took a look outside. Alexis—" He pins me with his sapphire eyes. "You're going to have to act like you know what you're doing, because trouble's coming."

My heart rate spikes at his tone. "Dragons? They're coming now?"

He shakes his head. "No, we didn't see them."

"But I checked from the sky and saw an angry mob headed our way, led by one of our favorite people," Tristan says. "Looks like we have a coup on our hands."

Gasps of surprise and worry fill the room. I snicker.

"Is that really such a big surprise?" I say when they all look at me. "I could feel it brewing before we left. Why do you think I'd planned to leave?"

More gasps and huffs come in response. Tristan levels an angry glare on me.

"It's not anyone from here," he grounds out through a clenched jaw.

"It's the same people who have always caused you problems," Owen says. "Julia and some of her henchmen."

"They'll be at our door in less than an hour," Tristan adds. "And from the pieces of conversation I picked up, Julia wants all of us ousted."

Something about this name and what they say make the hairs on the back of my neck bristle. Everyone else reacts in their own way, tension filling the air.

"Who the hell is Julia, and where did she and her henchmen come from?" I ask. "And why would she want to take over The Loft?"

"Not only The Loft, Alexis," Tristan says. "Everything. The Amadis. The world."

CHAPTER 15

I suppress a hysterical laugh. "What the hell does that mean? Who even thinks like that? *I want to take over the world.*"

"People like Julia," Sheree mutters.

"If you remembered, you'd understand." Vanessa leans her butt against the edge of a table and crosses her legs at the ankles. "But from what I've heard about Julia's friends, I wouldn't be surprised if one of them said exactly that. You yourself have called them power-hungry assholes."

"And am I a good judge of character?"

One side of her mouth lifts. "You chose us as your closest advisors, didn't you?"

"We need a plan," Tristan says. "We need to calm Julia and her people down before the dragons decide to attack. Our people are too weak to fight one, let alone both."

Everyone speaks at the same time, throwing out ideas. More than once someone mentions fighting the Amadis. Their own people. This debate grows more ridiculous by the minute.

"Everyone shut up!" I yell over them, and they actually do. The room falls deathly quiet as they all stare at me expectantly. Their thoughts that Blossom's antidote might be working slide into my mind, and I shake my head. No, I'm not back to the real Alexis, but at least I have their attention. "Look. Maybe this Julia has a point. In fact, give me one good reason why I shouldn't step down. Tell me why Tristan can't lead this place and you all be *his* advisors. He seems to be the one in control, anyway."

They all stare at me in shock and confusion, as though they've never heard anything more absurd. Tristan, however, growls with anger.

"The Angels chose *you*," Owen says. "You are the leader. Tristan is your second."

I wait for more explanation but he provides none. Nobody else does, either.

"That's *it*?" I scoff with disbelief. "These people accept me as a leader simply because some invisible Angels said so?"

He rolls his eyes. "No. Because you've proven that they're right."

"Ha! In what possible way? I've seen their memories. People have died! Their loved ones!"

Owen flinches at this, and guilt pricks my heart. Yet I continue.

"Someone *you* love is dead, too. This whole world is dead. Whether I'm at fault or not, which I don't know, that's what everyone else believes. And what they *believe* about their leader is all that matters. Nobody can lead without their people's trust. Or, at least, nobody will follow."

Vanessa blows out a huff and tosses her white-blonde ponytail over her shoulder. "I call bullshit. I don't know where the hell you got that from, but they follow you because you fight for what's right." She lifts her hand and jabs a finger at me in rhythm with her words. "Because even when *you* think you've given up, you haven't. You'll dig as deep as you need to to keep going, and they *know* that. They've *seen* it. They've seen your willingness to sacrifice *everything* for them and for what matters. They believe in you even when you don't believe in yourself."

"They don't blame you for what happened," Sheree pipes in. "None of us do. We all know loss is part of war. We're all grateful you did what was necessary so there still *is* a world. Grateful we're still here to continue fighting for it."

Vanessa leans closer to me, piercing me with those sharp blue eyes as she drums her finger against her temple. "Why don't you tap into every single person's mind to see for yourself? I guarantee that's what you'll find. And trust me, if I didn't believe it, I'd be the last person to blow smoke up your ass."

I lean forward, too, right up to her face. "I *have* listened to the thoughts of people here. They all blame me. That's exactly why I was going to leave. I probably should have when I had the chance."

Tristan lets out another growl and charges out of the room, slamming the door after him. The entire room shakes with the force, silencing everyone for a moment.

"Now you've done it," Carlie whispers.

"So what was your plan?" Vanessa demands. "Were you really going to take off so we had to tell *your* people that you bailed and abandoned them?"

"You wouldn't!" Blossom gasps.

"There's no telling what Tristan would do," Sheree says, a little more calmly than Vanessa or Blossom, though worry fills her tone. "But there would be total chaos here. Julia and her people would have no problem barging in and taking over before anyone knew what happened."

"And you guys would let them do that?" I ask in disbelief. So much for me being a good judge of character. "*You* wouldn't fight for what's right?"

"Of course we would, but Julia and the others have a way of putting us in the minority," Owen says. "She's convinced her way is the right way, and by the time she was done with the people, she'd have them brainwashed into thinking a penguin would be a better leader than you. They believe in you now, but if you choose to abandon them, you'll only be proving Julia right. And since we're *your* council, she'd kick us out, too."

I blow out a sigh. Everyone's aversion to this Julia leaves my own mouth tasting bitter. I certainly don't like agreeing with her that I'm the wrong leader, but I have a hard time believing what my council says about me. They're supposedly my friends, too. At least, Alexis's. And this close to finding an antidote, they'd probably say anything to keep me here. So I take a moment to listen to the nearby thoughts around us. Word of the coup has already spread like wildfire. And to my astonishment, their thoughts verify exactly what my council has said.

A speech in my voice, rallying warriors on the battlefield, echoes in one person's mind, and I can feel his pride in fighting with me. Another feels a mixture of admiration for the sacrifices I've made and anger that anyone would think of challenging me. As bad as things are with the water situation, he believes the small, tight-knit civilization at The Loft would crumble if this coup wins.

Does everyone here truly believe this? Or are these guys thinking the right thoughts, knowing I might be in their minds? That has to be it, because I've heard everyone's thoughts before. They aren't nearly as positive when they don't know I'm listening. As I spread my mind out further to listen to more, I start to wonder if Tristan is running around, telling everyone what to think. But why would he do that? It's not like he wants me here. I'm not even a good mother to his babies anymore—if I ever was.

He barges back into the room a moment later, the pixie grasped by the collar of her shirt in his large hand.

"Tell us the truth," he orders as he practically tosses her to the center of the room. She stands with her fists at her sides, but I detect the slight tremble to them. "You know something about this, don't you? About Julia?"

The pixie's bottom lip quivers. She slowly nods her head.

"She hired me to do this to Alexis," she whispers.

"*Julia* did?" Sheree asks with surprise.

"Oh my gosh! That's it!" Blossom practically squeals as she bounds for the door. "I had the intention all wrong."

"And what else?" Tristan snarls as Blossom disappears.

The pixie frowns, her whole body trembling. "She had me poison your water, too."

Vanessa takes a threatening step closer. "Why?"

Tristan answers for her. "To create chaos, of course. That's what faeries do best." The pixie doesn't deny it, only stands there, quaking as Tristan continues. "Julia needs to prove to whatever followers she has that we've lost control here."

"Which would mean we couldn't handle the Amadis or anything else the Angels asked of Alexis," Sheree adds, catching on.

Vanessa places her fists on her hips and cocks her head as she glares at me. "Well, then, we'll just have to prove that bitch Julia wrong, now won't we?"

As though in response, an alarm, a different sound than the water one, wails around us.

"They've crossed our wards," Owen says.

"What's the good of having wards if they can cross them?" I ask.

"They're Amadis. The wards are an alarm system for us, not a deterrent to our own kind," Owen says.

"Own kind, my ass," Vanessa mutters.

"Carlie, go take care of the people," Tristan says. "We need them well and strong, ready to fight in case it comes to that. Owen, Vanessa, Sheree, and Jax, come with me. Maybe we can shut Julia down before she even starts." He pins me with his gaze. "You stay here. We don't need to take any chances with them seeing you like this."

I repress the urge to make a face at him as he turns for the door.

Within a moment, everyone has cleared out of the room, once again leaving me alone, except for the pixie. She stares at me with huge eyes, her body still quivering with fear. I stare back at her while pondering the idea of walking up the tunnel and giving in to Julia's demands. There may be an adjustment period for everyone, but whether she'd be better at the job than me or not, giving up the stress and pressure is tempting. I can't imagine wanting the responsibility given to Alexis by the Angels. She—I—may have pulled the world through the big War of Armageddon and led them to victory, but the real work lies ahead. With or without my memories, I don't think I want the job. I also don't want to be the cause of any kind of fight with the Amadis outside.

Something about this Julia niggles at me, though. Perhaps it's what everyone has said about her and maybe some part of my own memory trying to push through, but I know in my gut that handing everything over to her isn't the right thing to do. Tristan can manage the responsibility, and maybe some of the council members . . . I think. But I can't leave them right now to deal with this mess I've somehow caused.

I spring from my seat, grab the pixie by the arm, and hurry for Blossom's lab, dragging the faerie with me.

"Please don't hurt me," she wails as I walk, pulling her along. "I'm on your side now. I broke my ties to Julia by telling you the truth, but she'll kill me if she finds out. You're supposed to be kind and protective, which is why I did it. You won't hurt me, right?"

"Who said I'm kind and protective?" I ask through clenched teeth as I turn down the hallway to the lab.

"Pretty much everyone."

"Yeah, well, I wouldn't know, would I? Thanks to you?"

"I'm so sorry. I really, truly am. I'm not used to this new Earth, and Julia found me and promised to take care of me, but then left me on my own in the woods. She said she'd come back for me when I did what she wanted, but she never returned. Then I heard about you and what you really did for everyone, and I hear the whispers in this place—my hearing's better than anyone here, including the vampires and the shifters, you know —and I know now I messed up. I don't want to be on your bad side. I was wrong. I admit it. And if you know anything about the fae, especially pixies, you don't hear that admission often. Please forgive me, my mistress?"

I peer down at her, and her head is lowered, her eyes peering up at me through her lashes.

"You can start showing your regret by ensuring Blossom has the right antidote this time," I say as I shove open the door to the lab and practically throw the green little thing at Blossom's feet.

Within a few minutes, they concoct what the pixie determines as the exact potion needed to restore my memories. I take the beaker and down the green, murky liquid that's much more bitter than any of the previous attempts.

And then we wait.

Yet nothing happens.

As the minutes tick by, Blossom and I grow more tense, our heads cocked, our eyes narrowing as we glare at the pixie who's backed herself up into the corner.

"It's the right recipe! I swear I don't know what's wrong!"

I shake my finger at her. "Do you value your life at all?"

She blanches, but before either of us can say anything, Tristan's voice booms in my head.

"Alexis, we need you to come out here."

But—

"You'll have to fake it! If you care at all, you'll pull off the best acting job you can muster. And bring whoever you can with you. They've pulled weapons and aren't backing down." He gives me a glimpse through his eyes of the scene around him—a couple hundred people surrounding my council.

After taking a deep breath to try to calm myself, I open up my mind to everyone in The Loft.

We're under siege. I know many of you are weak and unwell, but if you stand behind me, Tristan, and the rest of us, and you're able to fight at all, we need your help. Arm up and let's go.

I rush to our room to change into fighting leathers and grab my weapons, and then head toward the front tunnel. At first, I make the trek by myself, and doubt that I'm a true leader to these people seeps in again. My footsteps echo hollowly as they land on the stone floor, bringing on the familiar feeling of loneliness. But then Blossom joins me, and a moment later, a few others fall into step behind us. Then more. By the time we reach the bottom of the tunnel and begin making our way up, nearly half of the six hundred people of the community are behind us.

The doors open before we reach the top. Tristan, Owen, and the others slowly back their way in, blurs of spell-lights flashing toward and away from them. A mob pushes forward, trying to get past them and enter The Loft.

I unsheathe my swords from my back, expose my wings, and take off in a sprint. The sound of hundreds of pairs of running feet thunders from behind me.

CHAPTER 16

*W*e charge out the tunnel, pushing the coup back. Weapons clash, magic spells fly, and teeth snap and tear at flesh. Images of a much larger, much scarier battle flash across my mind. I squeeze my eyes shut then open them again in time to block a fist coming at my face. I swing around and catch a glimpse of figures flying in the sky toward us. Great. The dragons. We'll have two fights on our hands—two fronts, two snake heads . . . Something dings in the far corners of my mind, but I can't focus on it as another punch soars at me. My arm flies up to block it, followed by my foot that swings up, landing against my attacker's ribs. The raven-haired woman, with fangs out, hisses with the contact.

"You won't win, Julia," I say.

"We're more powerful than you think," she replies before lunging at me.

I spring into the air, jumping out of her reach, but she follows me, grabbing onto my ankles. My wings flap, taking us higher as I kick a foot free and plant my boot in her face. She falls back toward the ground at the same time a bright white light flashes across my vision, blinding me and making my head thunder. I tumble in the air after her.

"*She knows who I am.*" Julia's thoughts pop into my mind just as my vision returns.

I remember exactly who you are, I say as I swoop upward, out of her reach when she tries to grab me again. I push my wings against the air until I'm soaring high above the fight. The people of The Loft have Julia's coup surrounded, yet they continue to fight. Two more figures fly from the opposite direction of the dragons, one small and the other tiny. As they approach, I recognize Cam and Robin, in her falcon form. Hundreds of people follow them on the ground, charging for the fight.

"*We brought backup for you, Alexis,*" Cam calls out to me.

The moment of relief vanishes, immediately replaced by visions of the big war ripping through my mind again. The blood. The death. The loss even in victory. I remember it all, my whole life. I remember the attacks, the battles, what Lucas had done not only to my people but to all of humanity. I remember the faces of those we've lost along the way. So, *so* many people we knew and loved. Many more than the garden of trees could possibly hold. Many more deaths than any one person should know in a lifetime, yet we all know it very well.

And I know one other thing: We can't go through that again. I don't care if these people are *willing* to fight for me. Because there's no reason for it. No reason for the carnage. No reason to lose more of our own. We are all Amadis. All on the same side. And almost everyone here is following me.

I need to lead them.

And I need to do so the way I want to, the way I decided to many months ago—out of love, not fear.

"STOP!" I yell, my voice thundering over the land, and everyone does as their eyes lift up to me.

"NO! You're here to fight for me," Julia shrieks with desperation as she shakes one of her so-called followers. I recognize many of them—including former residents of The Loft, the scout groups who'd gone to sample the water and never returned.

I fly around in a tight circle about ten feet above everyone's heads. "We surround you. You're outnumbered. But it doesn't matter. Do we really need to be fighting each other? Haven't we seen enough of the horrors of war to last a lifetime? Haven't we done enough? Please, I ask you to stop fighting each other. Embrace each other as brothers and sisters, because that's what we are. We are family, not enemies!"

"We need a matriarch who cares about everyone, not just herself and those closest to her," Julia shouts as she turns a circle on the ground, trying to rally her people. "We need a *real* leader!"

"We have a real leader! We have Alexis," someone in the crowd yells, and hundreds of voices shout in support and begin to chant "A.K.'s Angels! A.K.'s Angels!"

"She's not a leader! She caused the deaths of thousands during the war," Julia counters. She spins to face my council, her dark eyes piercing Owen. "She caused the death of your—"

Owen's fingers clamp against his thumb, silencing Julia.

"No, you don't," he seethes as he takes a step closer to her, thrusting a finger in her face. "Don't you dare twist our losses to your benefit. The *Daemoni* killed them, and you know it, Julia. You know Lucas and the Daemoni caused it all, not Alexis. She did exactly what needed to be done. You're grasping at straws. Again. And this time you can't blame Kali for your—" Owen cocks his head and looks over at me. "What did she call it, Alexis?"

I feel a smile trying to form on my face at a memory of another faceoff with Julia. "Unbecoming behavior?"

"I was thinking more along the lines of what she'd said before the trial." He looks back at Julia. "You can't blame anyone else for your *filthy, traitorous lies*."

He snaps his fingers, and an audible gasp comes from Julia, but she says nothing in reply.

"Any other accusations you have against my wife?" Tristan asks, also advancing on her. She backs up, but the crowd behind doesn't let her through. The same crowd who'd come here in support of her. She certainly must have told them a mound of lies—or wiped out their memories.

Julia's dark gaze swings from Tristan's face to mine. "Tell us, *Ms. Alexis*." She sneers my name. Her fight hasn't dissipated yet. "What are you doing for the people now? Why aren't you out there helping rebuild like you claim you're supposed to be? Because of your lack of leadership, our world is in this state, and you're doing nothing about it. You act as though you don't even care! What have you been doing the last several days as more reports come in about problems around the world?"

I hover in the air right over her, raising my voice so everyone can hear me. "You know damn well what I've been doing, Julia. Fighting the poison *you* delivered. Two poisons, actually. One to me, another to my people. All so you could make us look bad. And you know why you needed to do that? Because you knew you had absolutely no justification for this coup."

I drop down in front of her, lowering my voice because what needs to be said next is only between her and me.

"You resent me because my grandmother loved me more than you. And despite how childish and ridiculous that is, you feel it anyway and you know it. Maybe instead of hating me so much for the love among family, you should ask yourself what it is about you that has kept you out of this family. Because, you know, we aren't all bound by blood. These people here —" I sweep my hand back to gesture at my council "—they're family to me. Just like they were to my grandmother. They've been brought into the fold. So why weren't you, Julia? That's what you should be asking yourself. Start with the shitty way you tend to treat all of us."

She glares at me, her mouth opening and closing like a carp because she has no defense for herself. I spring up again to address the crowd.

"This fight is over," I declare. "I am fine. We are all fine. And we will work *together* to do as the Angels have asked of us. ARE YOU WITH ME?"

A deafening roar fills the air, including from those who'd come with Julia. A lump jumps into my throat, and goose bumps rise on my arms as I feel the love from my people. I see it written all over every one of their faces. I feel their pride and hope in their cheers. They have such deep, heartfelt belief in me. They aren't only behind me, but they're *with* me.

I turn in the air and point my dagger toward the dragons. "Now, we seem to have a real fight on our hands."

The largest of the dragons, the one whose blood I had drawn only yesterday, flies closer to us, but then drops behind the hill. A moment later, a large, muscular man appears over it. He strides toward us, wearing nothing but what he'd been born in. His skin is pale and his head's topped with contrasting black hair. His eyes are the same royal blue in human form as they are in his dragon form. Although he's obviously unarmed, his clan hovers above us, with plenty of natural weapons. All of my people tense, ready to go to battle again.

"We are not here to fight you, Alexis," the man says, his voice deep, though not quite as deep as it had been in my head when he was in dragon form. He speaks with an Irish lilt. "We thank you for what you have done for our people, for our freedom. We will always remember that. But you should know we will not hesitate to protect what is ours, especially our young and our treasures. There is ample water in the lake for all of us, so consider that yours as well as ours. But anything else . . . you would do well to not test us."

With that, he bursts into a dragon and rockets into the air. He and the

KRISTIE COOK

others turn and soar away, toward the lake. Everyone below watches with held breaths until the magnificent beasts are out of sight. Weapons are re-sheathed, and everyone turns and greets each other like the long lost friends they are. Julia tries to slither away through the crowd, but Vanessa easily catches her.

I want nothing more than to be with my husband and my daughters. Although I've been with them all week, I don't really feel like *I've* been with them. But we have business to take care of first. I call my council, including Cam, to the conference room, along with Julia. The trial is a condensed version of the one Tristan and I had sat through a few years ago, but with the tables turned.

"Do you have anything to say for yourself?" Tristan asks Julia.

She looks up at me, her eyes much softer than they had been only moments ago. Her words are pleas rather than accusations. "I'm sorry. I know I went about this the wrong way, but to be honest, Ms. Alexis, I just want to matter again. I want to make a difference for the Amadis, like I did when I served your grandmother. I miss being on the council. If you could find it in your heart to give me back my old position, I promise to always serve you as loyally as I did Ms. Katerina."

I keep my face neutral as I study her, half-expecting her to drop to her knees and clasp her hands in front of her. But that would be going too far for Julia. I don't believe a single word she speaks. She can't possibly expect me to trust her. I try to, though. Keeping to my philosophy of leading out of love and not fear, I forgive her, and I put the decision up to a vote.

"It's unanimous," I say once everyone on the council states their vote. "You will never serve on this council, Julia. You will leave this place and not return. You will not attempt another overthrow, or next time, the consequences will be much more severe. I believe your idea of punishment is banishment from the Amadis. I'm giving you the benefit of the doubt this time, but next time, we'll do just that. Do you understand?"

She blinks rapidly as she nods, then she turns for the door.

"We'll escort her far, far away," Vanessa says with excessive glee in her voice.

Before I can sneak away with Tristan, I have one more task to take care of as leader of these people. I go back outside where everyone still gathers in a party-like atmosphere. I rise into the sky to gain their attention again, Tristan at my side now.

"I want to thank you all for supporting me, especially these last several

110

days that have been so harrowing. I know it hasn't always been easy, and there will be many more difficult times ahead of us. But we *are* a family. The Amadis are, and the people of The Loft are. We take care of each other. We have each other's backs. And we love each other."

"We are A.K.'s Angels!" someone yells with a hearty fist pump. Several cheers lift in reply, causing a smile to break out on my face.

"As for The Loft, we are in fine shape," I continue. "The lake is a prime water source, and as you heard, we won't have any problems from the dragons tapping into it. Our water availability should be back to normal in the next couple of days. You'll even be able to shower."

"Thank God!" somebody yells, and laughter fills the air.

I sit on the floor of our apartment, my back against the bed as Elliana feeds. My head falls back, my eyes close, and I smile from the bliss of knowing I can take care of my children, my family, my people again.

"Are you sure that hadn't been some weird dream?" I ask, not for the first time. My memories of my whole life are perfectly restored—except for the last few days. I mean, I remember the events, but I feel like I'd been a cartoon version of myself. Like I wasn't fully *here*, not the real me—not Psycho or Swirly Alexis of my past, but not Real Alexis either.

"Unfortunately, my love, it all happened, and you have no idea how good it is to have you back," Tristan says from my side. He'd just finished changing Brielle and plays with her as she lies on the floor, giggling.

"You have no idea how good it is to be back," I say. "I was really starting to think you could actually hate me."

He doesn't reply right away, and my heart skips. Could he really have?

"Never." The word is a breath on my lips, sweet and tangy. I open my eyes to find him right in front of me. He cups my face with one hand and leans in. His lips brush over mine, softly at first, but the kiss quickly escalates, bringing with it memories of a thousand other kisses and the love we've always shared. And I know that even if my memories hadn't returned, we would have found a way. Because we belong together, forever and always.

"Until the *end* of forever," I whisper.

"Until the end," he replies.

EPILOGUE

SIX YEARS LATER

*T*he storm explodes out of nowhere. It's been nearly seven years since the bombs dropped, yet their effects still wreak havoc around the world, causing insane weather and weird natural disasters. I'd hoped that by now we would have made more progress in rebuilding civilization, but the black magic storms that stir up nuclear fall-out keep most of the world underground.

Owen and some of the other mages have used potent magic to clear and protect an area around The Loft that allows our residents a respite from the underground life. The space now teems with people hurriedly packing things up and rushing down below.

"Alexis!" Teah runs toward me. I'd seen her shuffling children inside several minutes ago. "We can't find the girls!"

"Aren't they inside with Teal?"

She shakes her head. "She took the other children in while I went looking for the twins. I'm so sorry! I don't even know when they might have wandered off."

My gaze swings around the area that had been bustling not too long ago, but was now completely clear, the last of our people making their way through the wide doorway. I try not to panic. Surely they've gone inside with everyone else, and the teachers hadn't seen them. My girls have a habit of falling into their own private world, separating themselves from the other kids. All except one—Blossom and Jax's daughter, an unexpected addition to our extended family shortly after the Julia fiasco.

"What about Charleigh?" I ask.

"She's inside with Blossom," Teah shouts.

Then the twins have to be, too. Using my telepathy, I search for the girls' minds, but I don't sense them inside or anywhere outside either. At least, not within our boundaries. I make a mental announcement to everyone below, calling for a head count and to find the twins. One by one, the replies come back. No twins to be found.

A large, powerful male body suddenly appears by my side.

"What the hell happened?" Tristan yells.

Teah's eyes grow wide, her face blanching. "I'm so sorry."

"Just get inside," I tell her. "We'll find them."

Some of my council members run out of the entryway to The Loft just as Tristan and I both reveal our wings. With the storm brewing, we don't have time to do a locator spell.

"Owen and Vanessa, go north," Tristan orders. "Sheree and Aidan, go east. Alexis and I will take the rest."

Vanessa and Owen immediately take off. Sheree and Aidan both shift first, and they're off, Sheree on the ground and Aidan's stone body flying just above her. Tristan and I both take to the sky. He goes straight south while I head west, making wide sweeping arcs to see as much of the terrain below as possible.

Everything is still an ugly gray, making it difficult to distinguish objects on the ground. The wind whips at me as more lightning flashes off toward the north. I can no longer suppress the panic that fights its way from my chest into my throat as minutes pass by with no sighting, no word from the others. We're surrounded by wilderness, the nearest town, Ravenbury, over seventy miles away—not counting the dragon clan, and I really don't want to even think about them. Not when my girls are out here alone.

"Found them!" Owen's voice whoops in my head, at the same moment the wind suddenly dies and the thunder silences. I see my girls' faces through his eyes, and my heart immediately settles, especially when I see Sasha with them. She would protect them at all costs.

"Momma! Daddy!" Brielle and Elliana squeal, running to us as soon as Tristan and I drop to the ground. Closing our wings in and making them vanish, we each scoop one of the girls into our arms.

"Look what we did!" Brielle says from Tristan's embrace, gesturing toward Owen and Vanessa—or perhaps toward Sasha who stands behind them, her tail end toward us as she sniffs the air.

"What the hell is that?" I demand. "And what the hell is wrong with Sasha?"

She's grown to the size of a wolf, a low growl rumbling in her throat. The hairs on my arms rise to match hers, a reaction not only to her but to the shift in energy as I take a step closer.

"Looks like a portal," Tristan says.

"Something's definitely not right about it. It feels . . ." I shudder. "*Dark.*"

Tristan moves closer to me, his arm muscles tensing around Brielle. "I feel it, too."

"It's okay, Momma," Elli assures. "Our friends are there."

Brie nods her head enthusiastically. "That's why we made it. They want to come visit us."

Tristan and I exchange a glance, brows raised.

"Seal it, shield it, and cloak it," I order Owen. "We don't need anyone finding this. Then check on it tomorrow."

Sometimes the portals simply disappear. Maybe this one would, too.

Later that night, I head up the tunnel to go outside, claiming I need a moment of fresh air and peace. But really, something's inexplicably drawing me out there. I consider that my gut's telling me to check on that damn portal, but the theory doesn't feel quite right. I think it's something else. As I'm opening the first door, the ward alarms go off.

The sound for a threat—specifically, the sound for Daemoni.

I duck under and quickly shut that door and use my magic to raise the outside one just enough to roll under. Pulling my dagger out, I follow my senses, sprinting to the east. I stop dead in my tracks by the Memorial Garden and turn to see a tall, broad male figure standing under my favorite tree.

"Dorian?" I gasp.

"Hello, Mother." When he turns to look at me, his gaze glows a bright red, shocking me again.

I take a breath, trying to steady my heart. "Are you . . . back?"

He frowns. "I can never come back here." The glow in his eyes dims. "It's too late now. I can never be who you want me to be. You have to let me go. But it's not too late for my sisters. Protect them so they don't become like me."

"Of course," I answer automatically. "But it's never too late for you either. I'll always love you, Dorian. Until the end." I move closer to him, still surprised to feel the evil power emanating off of him.

Shaking his head, he reaches for me, and my heart leaps with hope. But then I watch as the last spark of light in his eyes snuffs out, leaving them dull, flat, dead.

"You have no idea what I've done, Mom. Let me go. I'm a monster now."

GLOSSARY & CAST

A reminder of who and what you've discovered so far in the Soul Savers world.

Aidan - Gargoyle shifter from Scotland.

A.K. Emerson – Alexis's famous pen name.

Alexis Ames Knight – Amadis matriarch. Married to Tristan Knight and mother of Dorian. Youngest daughter to ever go through the Ang'dora and to become matriarch. Her bio father is the leader of the Daemoni. Known abilities include telepathy, electricity, telekinesis, super strength, speed and senses, Amadis power.

Alys – Recently converted Amadis vampire.

Amadis (uh-MAH-dees) – Secret matriarchal society that serves as the Angels' army on Earth, currently led by Alexis Ames Knight. Their purpose is to defend human souls from the Daemoni and to convert Daemoni souls to Amadis. Consist of a variety of supernatural beings.

Amadis daughters – Women of the bloodline of the original creator of the Amadis. Each daughter eventually serves as the matriarch.

Amadis power – A special power of love and light gifted to the Amadis by the Angels. The Amadis daughters receive it during the Ang'dora. Other society members are granted a lower level of power upon conversion and official acceptance into the Amadis.

Ammi – Started the London cell of AK's Angels with her sister Kristen. Turned into a vampire and converted immediately by Char and Alexis.

Andrew – The Angel who fell from Heaven and fathered Cassandra and Jordan before eventually ascending (read about it in *Genesis: A Soul Savers Novella*).

Ang'dora – Literally means "gift of the Angels" (Ang = angels, dora = Greek word for gifts). An enigmatic change all Amadis daughters go through to receive their powers and supernatural abilities. Usually happens in middle age, after the daughter has experienced major milestones of life as a human, but Alexis went through it quite early. Except for Sophia, no Amadis daughter has given birth after the Ang'dora.

Angels – Spirits of Heaven who (primarily) remain in the Otherworld. Most fight in the age-old war with Demons, battling for human souls.

Armand – French vampire on Rina's council, he oversees Amadis police force and is anti-Tristan. Killed by Daemoni.

Attair – Amadis warlock from Arabia who's on Rina's council and is anti-Tristan.

Baby Cakes – Faerie who's a friend of Bree, so she's helped Tristan and Alexis. For a price, surely.

Blossom – Alexis's best friend and council member. Amadis witch from the Daytona coven.

Bree – Tristan's birth mother. Fae.

Brielle Sophia Ames Knight – Baby daughter of Alexis and Tristan, twin to Elliana, sister to Dorian. Currently an unknown creature with wings.

Brogan – Amadis vampire, turned when the Daemoni first came out to the humans during the war. After retiring from the military, he started The Prepper's Stash House, a multi-million dollar doomsday prep company, which turned out to be a really good thing for Alexis and A.K.'s Angels, who converted him to Amadis. He's much cooler than his nephew, James.

Cam - A summoned son, now an Earth's Angel

Carlie – Alexis's human classmate during her first year at college. Now a doctor in D.C.

Cassandra – Half angel, half human who started the Amadis (read her story in *Genesis: A Soul Savers Novella*).

Chandra – Amadis were-tiger and member of the matriarch's council who oversees the region of India.

Charlotte Allbright – Amadis warlock, Owen's mother, Sophia's best friend, and overall badass aunt figure to Alexis.

Cloak – A magic spell performed by mages that hides or makes invisible its subject. Often used in conjunction with a shield.

Conversion – The process of eliminating dark or light energy and replacing it with the opposite, then indoctrinating the supernatural being into the new society. The Amadis purpose is to convert Daemoni souls before they become damned, destroyed, or forever lost. However, on occasion, Amadis members will convert to the Daemoni (e.g., Ian).

Cruz – A Daemoni were-jaguar.

Daemoni (day-MAH-nee) – Satan's servants as the Demons' army on Earth, currently led by Lucas. They turn humans to harvest their souls and build their army. The Amadis try to stop them.

Debbie – Faerie in England who helps Alexis and Tristan from time to time. Cohorts with Stacey, another faerie.

Demons – Spirits from Hell, some being angels that fell from Heaven with Satan as his followers and others being his creations. They take various physical forms, including horned and winged beasts and possessors of human meat suits.

Dorian Knight – Son of Alexis and Tristan, unknown creature but currently human. Known abilities include self-healing and flying. Converting to Daemoni?

Dragons - One of the many creatures that had disappeared from this realm when they were captured by Satan and held prisoners in Hell

Earth's Angels – Newly created by the Angels, on the lowest rung of the Angel hierarchy, includes Alexis, Tristan, the Summoned sons who have converted back to Amadis, as well as their offspring. Alexis leads them.

Edmund – Summoned son and member of the Daemoni. Known abilities include flashing, super strength and speed, idiocy, and being an overall douche-canoe.

Elliana Katerina Ames Knight – Baby daughter of Alexis and Tristan, twin to Brielle, sister to Dorian. Currently an unknown creature with wings.

Ethan - Leader of the dragon clan closest to The Loft

Eris – Daemoni witch from ancient times who helped Jordan create the potion that changed everything (read about it in *Genesis: A Soul Savers Novella*).

Faeries/Fae – Little is known about the fae as they tend to stay away from human affairs, as well as those of the Amadis and Daemoni. A handful do enjoy wreaking havoc in the Earthly realm, and sometimes they may even help out. They're considered Otherworldly creatures, because their world is not exactly part of Earth. They closely guard their secrets about the Faerie realm.

Ferrer – Blacksmith mage who lives on Amadis Island.

Fertility Stone – The faerie stone Bree gave Tristan when he was a young boy, embedding it in his heart with the instructions to give it to his true mate. Only when she has possession of it can he father children. The stone also allows the holder to share their emotions so he could feel his mate's love—but also the possessor's darker emotions.

Flashing – The supernatural ability to transport to another location up to a hundred miles away (give or take) in the blink of an eye. While objects can be held or attached to the body during a flash, Tristan is the only known creature who can flash while carrying another person. While both Daemoni and Amadis can flash, it's not necessarily a natural ability for all —some creatures have to be assisted by mages.

Galina – Russian Amadis warlock and a member of the matriarch's council, she favors Tristan and Alexis.

Gargoyles - Little is known about them, as Aidan is the first to be seen in many centuries. They're somehow connected to the dragons.

Hades – Daemoni HQ, an underground city in the Taymyr Peninsula of Siberia.

Heather – Human girl, Dorian's babysitter and friend, daughter of Phil and sister to Sonya.

Hellfire – Direct from Hell, used by Demons, one of the few things that can scar, severely maim, and possibly kill Alexis and Tristan.

Hunters – Humans (or are they?) who know about the supernatural creatures and kill them.

Ian – Member of the Daemoni, converted from the Amadis. Known abilities include compensating for his minuscule junk by spilling secrets, causing problems with the Amadis, and ruining Alexis's life.

James – The boy Alexis punched in the nose when she was a teenager. Later became a hunter, and they met up again in D.C.

Jaxon – Were-croc from the Australian Outback who's become part of Alexis's team. Blossom's beau.

Jeana – Sorceress who tortured Alexis and Owen to learn Lucas and Kali's secret about the Norman soldiers. Mate of Merrick. Dead.

Jelani – Wizard from Africa who is one of the matriarch's council members.

Jessica – Faerie with a southern accent, calls Lisa her sister.

Jordan – Early leader of the Daemoni who sought power over all, inadvertently helping to create the Amadis (read his story in *Genesis: A Soul Savers Novella*).

Julia Acerbi – Vampire and Amadis matriarch's council member. She'd been one of Rina's closest advisors and friends.

Kali – Daemoni sorceress who took over Martin Allbright's body. Dead.

Katerina "Rina" Ames – Past matriarch of the Amadis. Known abilities included telepathy, super strength and speed, flashing, bonding souls, converting souls to Amadis, making ballgowns everyday attire. Ascended.

Kristen – Human girl who started the London branch of AK's Angels with her sister, Ammi.

Kuckaroo – Amadis village in Australia.

Lesley – Daemoni vampire. Companion of Sonya and Alys. Died in the war.

Lilith – Bree's daughter and Tristan's sister. Dead.

Lisa – Faerie with a southern accent, calls Jessica her sister.

Loft, The – Formerly The Prepper's Stash House, a massive underground nuclear bunker that had been the storehouse for the multimillion dollar doomsday prep and survival training company. Given to the Amadis by Brogan, the owner, after A.K. Angels arrived for shelter and converted him. Sarcastically renamed The Loft.

Lucas – Alexis's sperm donor and leader of the Daemoni. Often (but not always) uses the last name Emerson.

Lykora – An Angelic being that is extremely loyal and highly protective of its master. When in hidden form, looks like a small white dog, but when in defensive mode, can grow as large as necessary to protect, has a wolf head and body, tiger stripes on a white coat, and feathered wings.

Mages – The wide classification of supernatural beings that can wield magic, including witches/wizards, warlocks, and Sorcerers/sorceresses. These general sub-classifications are based on strength of power. Some may call themselves by other names, depending on the type of magic they use, preference, or other reasons (e.g., Shamans, Druids, etc.).

Martin Allbright – Powerful warlock, Charlotte's husband and Owen's father.

Merrick – Sorcerer who tortured Alexis and Owen to learn the secret about the stones that control the Norman soldiers. Jeana's mate. Dead.

Minh – Vietnamese witch, member of the matriarch's council, oversees the Asian region.

Molita – Daemoni born warlock converted to Amadis during the war.

Noah – Sophia's twin brother, Rina's son, a Summoned son with the Daemoni and controlled by Kali.

Norms/Normans – Normal humans.

Oliver Winston Chambers – Sophia's true love who was turned to a vampire then buried under a building in Charlotte, North Carolina, for a century. Dead again.

Ophelia – Witch who serves as head of staff at the Amadis matriarch's mansion.

Otherworld – Currently unknown but seems to refer to Heaven and Hell, as well as Faerie.

Owen Allbright – Warlock and Alexis's so-called protector. Also like a brother to her and Tristan's best friend. Known abilities include shielding, cloaking, magical bindings, flashing, and pushing everyone's limits.

Phillip Jones – Human wife beater, child abuser, and overall scum of the earth who drove an older orange Camaro. Heather and Sonya's father. Dead.

Pixies - A type of fae; small, spits pixie dust that can be toxic to those of the Earthly realm.

Portals – Magical doorways that can only be created and controlled by sorcerers/sorceresses and extremely powerful warlocks like Owen. They allow teleportation to anywhere in the world just by stepping through.

Rene – Daemoni were-cheetah who chases Alexis down in Hades.

Safe House – Homes, lodges, and other accommodations scattered around the world where Amadis can retreat to when under attack or when going through the conversion or transformation process.

Sasha – Dorian's lykora, now loyal to the twins.

Satan – No explanation necessary.

Savio – Italian were-shark who was on Rina's council and was anti-Tristan.

Seth – Tristan's former name when he was Daemoni. The Daemoni still call him that.

Sheree – An Amadis were-tiger who'd been bitten and turned against her will by the Daemoni. She was Alexis's first ever conversion from

Daemoni to Amadis. Now she helps with conversions of others and is a close friend to Alexis.

Shield – A magic spell performed by mages that puts a protective barrier around its subject. If the subject is not also cloaked, the subject can still be seen, so it's often used in conjunction with a cloaking spell.

Shihab – Wizard from Arabia who sat on Rina's council.

Solomon – Vampire, Katerina's partner, and Amadis council member. Known abilities include being scary AF. Dead.

Sonya – Recently turned vampire, now converted to Amadis. Heather's sister. A.K. Emerson's "biggest fan" (a/k/a stalker).

Sophia Ames (a/k/a Mom a/k/a Mimi) – Alexis's mother and Amadis daughter. Known abilities included telekinesis, summoning and manipulating water, persuading others to do as she likes, sensing the truth of a situation, super strength and speed, flashing, converting souls to Amadis. Ascended.

Sorcerers/Sorceresses – The most powerful of the mages that can boost their energy by siphoning more from the earth and everything around them. Their greed for power, narcissism, and general disdain for pretty much everyone make them loners and also not part of the Amadis.

Stacey – A faerie in England who helps Alexis and Tristan from time to time. Cohorts with Debbie.

Stefan – Warlock, council member, and Sophia's former protector. Known abilities included creating a protective shield, flashing, serving as Alexis's only father figure. Dead.

Summoned Sons – Amadis sons, twins of Amadis daughters/matriarchs, who always go to the Daemoni, as though magically summoned. Include Noah, Edmund, and Dorian.

Sundae – Alpha of the Georgia wolf pack. Trevor's mate.

Sylvie (Aunt Sylvie) – Blossom's aunt and leader of the Daytona Beach witch coven.

Teah & Teal – Human cousins who'd joined A.K.'s Angels in Florida with Heather and Sonya. Teachers at the school in The Loft.

Trevor – Amadis werewolf and leader of the main Florida wolf pack. Sundae's mate.

Tristan Knight – Former Daemoni converted to Amadis by Sophia. Matriarch's second, best friend, and husband. Dorian's dad. Sexy AF warrior. Known abilities include shooting fire from his palm, quickly determining the best solution if he knows enough of the facts, telekinesis, paralysis, instant killing power, super-duper strength and speed, brooding with guilt, giving a girl multiple Os.

Vampires – Supernatural beings that are sustained by blood. They can also feed on fear and other emotional energy. There are vampires on both the Amadis and the Daemoni sides.

Vanessa – Formerly one of the Daemoni's star vampires recently converted to Amadis. Alexis's half-sister, Victor's twin, and Lucas's daughter. Known abilities include stirring up trouble and pissing everyone off.

Veil – The magical barrier between the Earthly realm and the Otherworld. Beings in the Otherworld can often see through the Veil to the other side, but those on Earth cannot see into the Otherworld. Well, except for those with the sight, but the talent is very rare.

Victor – Vanessa's twin brother, Alexis's half-brother, Lucas's son and Daemoni vampire who's not too bright.

Warlocks – Part of the mage classification, supernatural beings who are born with the ability to wield magic and physically endowed with strength and speed, making them excellent warriors. They are not gender specific and are on both the Amadis and Daemoni sides.

Whitby Abbey – Ancient abbey on the northeastern coast of England. The place where Dorian was found, where Alexis faced off with Lucas, and where Sophia, Rina, and Winston died.

Witches/Wizards – Part of the mage classification, supernatural beings who are born with the ability to wield magic, usually using a wand as well as spells, incantations, potions, elemental energy, etc. While they can be quite powerful, their powers and physical strengths aren't as strong as Warlocks or Sorcerers. Using the term Witch or Wizard was traditionally by gender, but really is up to each individual's preference. There are Witches and Wizards on both the Amadis and Daemoni sides.

Were-creatures/animals (a/k/a Shifters) – Supernatural beings with two combined spirits—human and animal—and they can physically shift between their two forms. There is a were-creature/shifter for nearly every predatory species on Earth, and they're on both the Amadis and the Daemoni sides.

Zombies – Reanimated corpses with deadly bites. Created by mixing necromancy magic with fatal and highly contagious viruses, such as Ebola. Lucas made them as an experiment and to provide meatsuits for the Demons he planned to let loose on Earth.

ABOUT THE AUTHOR

Kristie Cook is a lifelong, award-winning writer in various genres, primarily New Adult paranormal romance and contemporary fantasy. Her internationally bestselling, award-winning Soul Savers Series includes seven books, as well as several companion novellas and short stories. Over 1.2 million Soul Savers books have been downloaded. She has also written The Book of Phoenix trilogy, a New Adult paranormal romance series. Her books have been featured in *USA Today's* HEA section, on Good Morning America, and in the Emmy's Gifting Suite.

Kristie also created, writes in, and publishes the award-winning Havenwood Falls shared world, a collaborative project with multiple series, dozens of authors, and countless stories.

Besides writing, Kristie enjoys reading, cooking, traveling, getting her hippie on, and feeding her addictions to coffee, chocolate, cheese, and her latest TV obsession. She has lived in eleven states, but currently calls Florida home.

CONNECT WITH ME ONLINE

I love to hear from and connect with readers. Please don't be shy.

Facebook Reader Group: https://www.facebook.com/groups/ClubKC.KristieCook

Email: kristie@kristiecook.com

Author's Website & Blog: http://www.KristieCook.com

Facebook: http://www.facebook.com/AuthorKristieCook

Goodreads: https://www.goodreads.com/KristieCook

Instagram: http://instagram.com/kristiecookauth

BookBub: https://www.bookbub.com/authors/kristie-cook

Word of mouth is very important for any author. If you enjoyed the book, please consider leaving a review, even if it's only a sentence or two. This is one of the most important and appreciated things you can do for an author.

ACKNOWLEDGMENTS

This book first released as *Awakened Angel* over a year after I thought the Soul Savers series had ended with *Fractured Faith*. By the time I finished that seventh book, though, I knew there was more to the story of Alexis, Tristan, their children, and the rest of their family. *Awakened Angel* was supposed to be the bridge to the new world after the war. It took several years, a lot of false starts, and a few breaks to finally realize where the story goes next—quite differently than I'd first thought. In fact, the next major storyline follows the next generation in the spinoff series, Knights of Souls and Shadows. However, I thought my readers deserve that bridge. So here we are, republishing *Awakened Angel* as the first part of the Age of Angels mini-series.

The years from when *Fractured Faith* published up until this epiphany have been a tumultuous period in my life. I wouldn't still be here, let alone writing, if not for some very special angels. As always, I thank my Creator first, for Making me who I am. Next, I hold an enormous amount of appreciation for my parents and my bonus parents, including my aunt and uncle, for supporting me in every way they possibly could so I wouldn't give up when life seemed especially and inescapably dark.

I also thank my friends, most of them authors and/or readers, who have been there with me through it all. I'm so grateful for my Havenwood Falls peers who have become such close friends while building that world, and now they support me as I return to my writing roots, which never would have happened without Havenwood Falls and Sun & Moon

Academy. Special gratitude goes to Belinda Boring, E.J. Fechenda, Rose Garcia, and Tish Thawer, amazing authors who've made a huge difference in my life. I'm so thankful for you all.

Much appreciation to my Crew, especially Stacey Nixon, Heather Wakefield, and Marissa Fagan, who have been the best cheerleaders a girl (and a writer) could ask for. Thank you to my reader group, Club KC, for insisting I write more Tristan and Alexis. You were right, but I really can't wait for you to get to know their children better. I hope you love the Age of Angels mini-series. I *know* you will love Knights of Souls and Shadows. Thank you again for spending your precious time in my worlds.

www.ingramcontent.com/pod-product-compliance
Lightning Source LLC
Chambersburg PA
CBHW021207130626
46554CB00005B/2023